The Circle of Life

The Circle of Life

Christine Paul

Writers Club Press
San Jose New York Lincoln Shanghai

The Circle of Life

All Rights Reserved © 2002 by Christine Paul

No part of this book may be reproduced or transmitted in any form or by any means, graphic, electronic, or mechanical, including photocopying, recording, taping, or by any information storage retrieval system, without the permission in writing from the publisher.

Writers Club Press
an imprint of iUniverse, Inc.

For information address:
iUniverse, Inc.
5220 S. 16th St., Suite 200
Lincoln, NE 68512
www.iuniverse.com

This is a work of fiction. All events, locations, institutions, themes, persons, characters and plot are completely fictional. Any resemblance to places or persons, living or deceased, are of the invention of the author.

ISBN: 0-595-22870-4

Printed in the United States of America

**FOR MY MOM,
VERNA (MOLINE) ANDERSON—
the Evelyn in my life.**

*Two of the most important things
that Mom has taught me are these:
When you want to escape life,
you can always lose yourself in a good book.
But when you must face it head-on,
you can only lose yourself in God.
Life is simply too unpredictable
to live it any other way.*

*My words are inadequate, Mom,
but this book says "I love you."*

*I think that when we breathe our last,
our fondest memories of our past
will be a lover's warmest kiss,
a baby's clenching little fist,
and arms that held us safe and close
when we needed them the most.
And if it's God we've loved the best,
we'll find our lives hold no regrets.*

——Excerpt from Nell Justison's Diary

Preface

About the Cover: *Is it a sunrise or a sunset? Like all things in life, your answer will depend on your perspective. Are you facing east at the dawn of a bright new day where you can envision your entire wondrous life stretching before you? Or are you facing west at the dusk of a day where you can savor the glorious details of a life lived well? Or perhaps you'll see it as both a sunrise and a sunset. For shouldn't we carry both perspectives in the circle of life?*

Acknowledgements

Special thanks to my writing and reading friends—Jim Oddie, Gail Wheeler, Janet Huhn, and Kathy Anderson—for input along the "Circle" way.

And thanks to Lisa Crayford of Country Gallery, Kimball, Minnesota, for the author's photograph.

Chapter 1

"Ashes to ashes. Dust to dust…"

Pastor Eric Masterson's resonant voice continued with the words that Evelyn Justison had always found to be of such comfort at a time like this. They assured her that death was a normal event in life, universal to all. Surely the words had cloaked her in a blanket of warmth and security when her Edward had passed on five years before. But now they only left her feeling cold and numb. And although it was only the second Wednesday in April of 1993, the weather wasn't the reason. It was a gorgeous, mild spring afternoon in central Minnesota.

Evelyn was seventy-five years old. The same age as her sister-in-law Nell had been. Life was too short. Or was it too long? It was too long, she decided. She should've passed on before dear Nellie.

"Mom? Are you all right?" Susan's worried whisper intruded.

Evelyn took a fortifying breath. There'd be plenty of time to contemplate life and death when she returned home to her lonely house. "I'm fine, dear," she said and patted her daughter's hand where it rested warmly on her shoulder.

"Mrs. Justison?" Pastor Masterson's slim, six-foot frame stood tall before her. His blonde hair lent him a cherubic appearance that defied his forty-three years, but his kind blue eyes seemed far older. "We're ready to…I mean, would you like to place a flower on the casket before it's—?"

"Let Susan lay the first flower there."

"Oh no, Mom. You and Aunt Nell were like sisters. You go ahead."

She turned and stared up into her daughter's brown eyes—Justison eyes—so like Nellie's, so like Edward's. "We'll do it together then."

But when they stood side by side, each holding a yellow rose that they'd pulled from the casket's floral bouquet, Evelyn waited until Susan had laid hers to rest there before laying down her own. It was right. No one on earth had meant more to Nell than Susan. The envy that she'd hidden for years welled up again unbidden. And on its heels, Evelyn felt the irony of it all. For what did she have to feel jealous of Nell any longer? Would she rather be dead? A good question. She'd have to table that also to consider when she returned home.

A short while later in the ladies' restroom at the Lutheran church in Crow River, Evelyn silently stared at her reflection. No tears had fallen to mar her carefully applied rouge. She'd cried enough over the past three days that there were simply no tears left. Her blue gray eyes looked lifeless. Evelyn patted her soft white hair into place, then hastily applied a bit of lipstick. She still looked like a corpse. Leaning closer to the mirror, she stared intently at the old woman who stared back. Where had all the years gone? Life was too short.

"Mom?" Susan burst in. "Are you all right?"

"Yes, dear. I'm just fine. But how are you holding up?"

"Oh, you know me. I deal with things in my own way."

"Sweetheart, you need to cry. I haven't seen you cry yet." Susan was still beautiful for a woman approaching forty. Her dark brown hair, bobbed short, enhanced the perfection of her oval face and bore only a few silver strands. She looked so feminine and pretty when she dressed up and used a little makeup. It was a shame she didn't do that more often.

"I've cried, Mom…at home when I'm alone. I just can't anymore. Besides, there are so many of Nell's friends and former students here." She beamed a smile. "Everyone loved Nell. They'll be looking for us to extend their condolences. C'mon. Let's go see them."

Evelyn allowed Susan to escort her into the noisy fellowship hall. The Lutheran serving ladies were bustling from the kitchen on their left to the rows of tables. They carried steaming bowls of goulash, jiggling dishes of Jello in every color of the rainbow, and plates laden with pieces of cake in an assortment of flavors. Buttered bread, dill pickles, and coffee servers waited on each table.

Pastor Masterson signaled them across the din to sit with him at the far end. Several people stopped them to offer their sympathies as they made their way across the expanse. When they finally reached the pastor, he held out the chair beside him on the end and seated Evelyn. Then he turned to seat Susan across from him, but she hastily sat without his assistance.

"Pastor, that was a beautiful service," Evelyn began. "I'm sure Nell loved it. So full of peppy songs and such an upbeat message."

He smiled. "I hadn't known Nell long, but I figured she wouldn't stand for anything less."

"You're absolutely right. Nell loved life. She didn't like to spend too much time feeling sorry for herself and wouldn't have wanted us to either."

"Susan." He directed his gaze across to her and smiled amicably. "You look a bit different than you did three days ago when we first met."

She accepted his teasing comment good-naturedly. "Is that a polite way of saying that I don't look like a handyman?"

He reddened. "My apologies again. It seemed like an honest assumption at the time."

"Apology accepted." She grinned. "Now, I'm starved. Pastor, would you pass the goulash?"

Evelyn smiled as she watched Susan settle her napkin across her lap. Apparently she remembered a few of the social graces that she'd taught her.

While they ate, Pastor remarked that he was very satisfied with his move to Crow River six months earlier. The town of five thousand was a far cry from the Minneapolis suburbs where he'd served at four different parishes over the course of seventeen years.

"Have you always been a city boy, Pastor?" Evelyn asked.

"Yes, but I've hesitated to make it well-known that I'm not Minnesota born and bred. Actually, I grew up near Chicago."

"Oh? What made you decide to seek a call in Minnesota?"

His smile faded, and he glanced down at his plate. "Ah…my wife was from Minneapolis. We…ah…met at college, and when we married she wanted to move back here."

"Well, that's a lucky thing for us." Evelyn hastily switched the subject to ease his discomfort. Although the specifics weren't known, the parishioners knew that his wife had been killed in some sort of automobile accident.

"And how does your wife like the rural life here?" Susan asked innocently.

His hurt gaze abruptly swung to her.

Susan paled and cast them both an apologetic expression. "I'm terribly sorry, Pastor. I remember now that Mom mentioned once that you were a widower. I simply forgot…I mean it slipped my mind. As you know, I don't come to this church, and I—"

"It's all right, Susan. I understand. There's no reason you should have remembered something you heard in passing, especially under these circumstances."

"But I still feel terrible. How long has it been…I mean when did she—?"

"My wife died a year and a half ago." Noticing Susan's discomfort, he waved his hand. "It's all right. You don't have to offer any words. I can see you feel embarrassed. Let's change the subject."

Evelyn broke in with a request to Susan for the cake tray. She selected a small piece of German chocolate and passed the tray to the pastor.

Like a godsend to end an uncomfortable moment, Hattie Carlson's brisk voice came from behind as she maneuvered her wheelchair alongside the table. "Well, Evelyn. We'll certainly miss old Nell, won't we?"

"That we will, Hattie. Especially you. I know that you and Nell did a lot of fun things together recently."

Hattie was close to Evelyn's own age and had been confined to her wheelchair for three years. She was one of those rare people who didn't let life's hardships break her spirits. A tall, thin woman with gray hair wrapped in a bun, her seated posture didn't diminish her straight-backed and regal appearance. And the ever-present twinkle in her green eyes testified to her sense of humor. Evelyn didn't know Hattie well, but to know her was to love her.

Hattie guffawed. "Oh yes. Nell and I had quite the great times." She leaned toward Evelyn conspiratorially but spoke loudly behind her concealing hand. "I'd tell you all about them if the pastor weren't eavesdroppin'." She winked.

He smiled good-naturedly. "I certainly appreciate your concern for my sensibilities, Hattie."

She turned to Susan. "Last time I saw you, you were just a tiny little thing. Susan, right? Nell told me you were a chip off the Justison block." She extended her hand.

Susan shook it. "If you mean that I'm ornery and opinionated like my dad and Nell were, then yes, I'm a chip all right."

Hattie guffawed and slapped her on the back. "My kinda gal. Say? Any objection if I invite your ma here over to the home so I can corrupt her?" She again shielded her mouth with her hand. "You didn't hear that last part, Pastor."

He raised his hands in surrender. "Selective hearing is one of my many sensibilities."

"Good. Good. So what'da'ya say, Susan?"

"Be my guest. Mom's a big girl." She glanced at Evelyn's petite frame and added, "Well, her heart's big anyway."

Hattie spun toward Evelyn and gasped. "You got heart problems too?"

"Well...no. I think Susan meant—" She ceased her explanation the instant she spotted the gleam in Hattie's eyes.

"Now you're catchin' on, Evie." She punched her arm. "You just can't take me too seriously. I'm full of bull most of the time. You didn't hear that last part either, Pastor."

He shook his head.

"So," she continued to Evelyn, "when can you come to the home and see me?"

"I...I...don't know. When would it be convenient?"

"They frown on visitors after 8:00 p.m., though I've been known to sneak 'em in later than that. (You didn't hear that last part, Pastor.) So for the sake of wrapping this up, why don't you come Friday at about two o'clock."

"In the afternoon?"

Hattie chuckled. "You're catchin' on. Yep. Two in the afternoon."

"O...okay."

With a whirl of her chair, the woman was off to hound another victim. Evelyn felt as though she'd been pole-axed. She hated the home. It was so depressing. Her fondest wish was that she'd expire before being forced to live there. Hattie Carlson should've been a salesman the way she'd just been railroaded.

"Dynamic, isn't she?" Pastor asked.

"I'd say *dynamite* would be a more apt description." At least she certainly packed an explosion.

An hour later, Susan drove her pickup up Evelyn's driveway. The stately white two-story house looked inviting. A nursing home could never beckon like that. Why, Evelyn could almost picture little Susan spilling out the front door to welcome her home with giggles and hugs.

"Mom? Are you all right?"

"Hmm? Fine, dear. I was just remembering."

"I'll carry the floral arrangement and the cards inside. You wait here for me to come back and get you."

"I'm not an invalid for heaven's sake. I can go in unaided."

"I know." Susan held her gaze. "Maybe I need you to lean on me once in a while."

"Oh honey." Evelyn cupped her cheek. "I lean on you all the time. You're always as close as the telephone. You come whenever I call. I...I hate to be a burden sometimes."

Susan's brown eyes were moist with emotion. Her face swam through Evelyn's own tears. "Love is never a burden, Mom."

Evelyn was touched deeply by that tender statement. But as she hugged Susan tight, she wondered briefly if it was true. Was love never a burden? She'd have to ponder that later.

"Would you like me to stay the night?" Susan stood inside the front door after she'd unloaded the pickup. "I could take my old room or even crawl in bed with you?"

Oh, that was tempting, Evelyn thought. To play at being a mother to her little girl again—completely needed, completely revered, completely trusted. But no. There came a time when a person outgrew make-believe games. Evelyn needed solitude more than anything tonight. She needed to think. "That sounds wonderful, dear, but I'm so tired I'm sure I'd turn in long before you anyway."

"Can I help you with anything?"

"Not today, honey. But I'll be sure to call you when I need you."

"Promise?"

Evelyn nudged her out the door. "I have your number, dear."

She watched as Susan backed out of the driveway before pulling the shade down. It was only five o'clock in the afternoon. The daylight grew longer with each day at this time of year. It would be hours before dark. Good. She hated the dark. Funny, how a house full of life could feel cozy on a dark night. But a house full of death felt cold.

She moved through the dining room toward the kitchen at the back. The oak woodwork and built-in china hutch were the things she'd fallen in love with when Edward had first found this house. They moved in as soon as the deal could be closed when they'd returned to Crow River from their two-year hiatus in San Francisco. Susan had been just a baby. It would be hard for Susan to part with this place when Evelyn died. Maybe she'd decide to sell her own home and would take up residence here.

The large box on the kitchen table was filled to the brim with sympathy cards. Evelyn ran her hand through them. "Oh Nell. You had so many friends for being a single lady all your life."

Would there be many people at her own funeral? Evelyn wondered. Certainly there'd be the members of her congregation…at least those who didn't work during the weekdays, assuming that her funeral was held on a weekday. On second thought, that didn't matter. Those who worked didn't usually attend a Saturday funeral anyway. So maybe the church members wouldn't lend a great audience to the occasion after all.

"Listen to me. Does it matter? If I'm dead, will I even care anymore how well-attended my funeral is?" Not one bit, she decided. Oh, how wonderful that will be—to be free of all the social conventions that life places upon us. To no longer feel any shame or fear, sadness or…guilt.

But that was water under the bridge. She had made peace with the guilt long ago. God's will wasn't always wrought in an understandable or even easily acceptable manner. But it was wrought nevertheless. Of that she was certain. Of that she was convicted. He'd given her that assurance long ago.

So now she had only to look back on her life and ask herself if she was satisfied. In order to do that, perhaps she should ask herself the converse. With what was she dissatisfied? Evelyn sank into the chair opposite the kitchen window and stared absently at the backyard. She wished that she'd been able to have a career like Nellie had. To have a place to dress up and go to each day where people missed you when you weren't there. She wished that Susan would've married and given her another baby to hold again. A child to mold and cherish and love.

She wished that Edward would've lived longer to share the loss of Nell—their Nell, who'd made both of their lives the richer.

She dropped her head to her folded arms on the table and wept, right at the base of the big box of cards.

Chapter 2

▼

"Lord, forgive me for my wastefulness, but I'm sure you understand." Pastor Eric Masterson hit the switch on the garbage disposal and gave a satisfied smile as it roared to life, digesting its contents.

"More of Miss Culpepper's hotdish?" his thirteen-year-old daughter, Kimberly, asked as she passed him.

"Yep. All gone. It's a shame."

"Can I fix you something you like to eat?"

"Actually, I'm not very hungry. The lunch after the funeral was pretty good and filling. They sent some of that home too. I'll heat some up for you."

"I can do that, Dad."

"No. That's all right. I don't mind." He opened the refrigerator, removing and stacking the foil-wrapped containers on the kitchen table.

Kim halted his movements with a hand on his arm. "Dad. I'm old enough now. I can do it."

She was still such a small, fragile-looking little girl. Her blonde hair was long and wavy like Sharon's had been. When he looked into her green eyes, he was again reminded of his wife. Even her poise, her cheerfulness, and her agreeable nature were constant reminders. Already she was maturing. Soon she'd be a woman with all the complications that would impose. How would he be able to handle that?

He absent-mindedly watched her scoop some of the goulash onto her plate and place it in the microwave. Hotdish of one sort or another. Every night. And she never complained. So much like her mother that way. But her mother would've prepared meat, potatoes, and vegetables—a balanced meal that wasn't all piled together. The ladies of the church were well-meaning in their efforts to keep them fed, but their menu was tiring.

The doorbell chimed, interrupting Eric's reverie. He moved to answer it.

"Good evening, Pastor," Debra Culpepper greeted him.

She was in her late thirties, tall, and a bit too slender. Her red hair had recently been cut and shaped into a style that framed her overly round face in an unappealing way. But her smile was very appealing, and she beamed it now. "Hello, Miss Culpepper. Is there something you forgot again?"

Her blush darkened her freckles. "Not this time. I…I was just wondering if you'd noticed that I arranged the pantry. I…I mean if there's anything you can't find, I could explain how I organized it."

"To tell you the truth, I haven't even set foot in the pantry in a long time. All you ladies keep us so well-fed that there's no need to fend for ourselves."

Debra giggled and blushed. Then noticing her empty casserole dish beside the sink, she smiled broadly. "You finished the oyster hotdish already?" she asked in astonishment.

"Ah—" He hated to lie.

"My. You must like oysters as much as I do."

Actually they made him queasy.

"I'll have to make sure that I whip up another batch for you tomorrow."

Eric glanced toward his daughter, hoping she'd bail him out, but Kim and her dinner plate had disappeared. "Ah…no, no. Please, Miss Culpepper, don't trouble yourself. We have quite a bit of delicious food in the house already. The funeral, you know, today."

"Oh yes. Nell Justison. That was such a shock. She was such a lively woman. I still can't believe it."

She was staring intently into his face. "Ah...yes. Happens to the best of us, I guess. She'll certainly be missed."

"Well," she said with the finality of one who had dismissed the subject. She hiked up her sleeves. "Let's get to the pantry. Shall we?"

Before he could respond, she was already opening the door and leading the way. He followed.

"Now, I took the liberty of stocking in some pasta products when they were on sale this week. Shells, rings, corkscrews, broad noodles, thin noodles, spaghetti noodles." She tapped the top of each box with her fingernail as though she were counting off tin soldiers. "And right next to them, you'll see I've put the soups and sauces that accompany them. Mayonnaise, hollandaise, tomato, cream of mushroom, cream of chicken, cream of broccoli, cream of asparagus, and spaghetti sauce."

Eric's head was swimming. Where had all this food come from? Had it been here all along or had she been putting every dime she earned by cleaning his house into these groceries? He decided not to ask. But this was getting out of hand. Was she pretending to be his wife? He'd have to do something. But what? He'd have to think.

"Fruit juices are here. Vegetable juices are here. Cereal products are on this shelf."

Her voice droned on, her finger tapping in cadence with the beat that was beginning to throb in his head. This had to stop. He couldn't take much more. He'd better evict her now, before he snapped and said something that would hurt her feelings. "Ah...Miss Culpepper—"

The tedious monologue stopped abruptly. She turned worshipful eyes upon him. "Oh Pastor. You can call me Debbie."

"Ah...Debbie then. I'm overwhelmed by what you've done in here." That much was certainly true. He turned and moved through the pantry doorway and into the kitchen. She followed. "And I'm certain that I'll be able to navigate my way through everything just fine. You've done such an excellent job of organizing, how could I not?" His hand on the kitchen doorknob, he stopped to smile at her, then opened the door.

Her red lashes fluttered and she blushed.

"But I really appreciate your taking the time to come here to explain. It was very thoughtful. Now I hope you'll have a pleasant evening."

She took his hint, giggling, and stepped through the doorway and onto the rear porch. "Thank you, Pastor. Any time. You have a nice evening too."

Eric softly closed the door behind her and wearily leaned his forehead against it. There was no doubt that he and Kimberly had needed to move after the accident. The mourning there had just never seemed to end. Every face he looked at in his old parish had reminded him of Sharon...or of Kyle. Both his wife and his fifteen-year-old son had been killed that fateful night in October 1991. And since they had both touched the congregation in some way, Eric knew that whenever the parishioners looked upon him or Kimberly, they were reminded of them too. It had been like living in a perpetual cycle of grief there.

But had it been wise to move, instead, to such a small town? A widower here seemed to be such an oddity that the whole town felt compelled to remedy the situation. And there wasn't a move that he made that didn't seem to become common knowledge through the finely grafted gossip grapevine. It was a good town, a friendly town, a concerned town. But couldn't a person be suffocated by too much goodness, too much friendliness, and too much concern?

He turned from the door. Kimberly had cleared the table of all the foil-wrapped containers. They were neatly stacked in the refrigerator again. She must've taken her dinner upstairs to her room to eat. She was probably working on homework or maybe relaxing and watching television there. Her room was her haven. Kim cherished her solitude.

Eric walked through the dining room and living room to his study off the front foyer. He'd have to write his Sunday sermon but not tonight. Tonight he felt the need for some solitude himself. Funerals always made him feel that way.

He wearily sank into the leather desk chair and swiveled it to face the window. The setting sun set the western sky on fire. A cacophony of birds, now rejuvenated from the inactivity of winter, sang their praise for its magnificence. Such glory to be had just from the object around which the earth orbited. How much greater heaven must be.

With a start, Eric realized that he hadn't felt so peaceful following a funeral service since before Sharon and Kyle's. Why was that? He'd conducted at least ten of them since then. What had been different about this one?

He recalled Mabel Walker's funeral at his former parish, shortly before he'd moved to Crow River. Eric had come home from it feeling especially unsettled. In fact, he'd written a sermon that night that had never been preached. It had been too bitter, too full of anger. Why had he done that?

Mabel had been ninety-one years old and had been living in a home for six years. The final year, she was usually sleeping when he visited her. If she was awake, she didn't even seem to recognize him. But he remembered her as being an especially sweet lady—the kind who seldom complained and usually looked on the bright side of her circumstances.

She had one child, a daughter who was about sixty when Mabel died. What had her name been? Maxine, he recalled. Maxine had insisted on the most somber of services—droning hymns and a reading from Lamentations. What person in their right mind chose a reading from Lamentations for a funeral service? It had to be the most depressing book in the Bible. But he had honored her wishes and then spent hours writing a sermon that would put a more upbeat swing on the text. It had hardly been worth the effort. Maxine had sat in the front pew and wailed through the entire thing, from the opening welcome to the retreat of the casket.

What reason had she had to carry on so? Yes, her mother had died. Granted, that was a traumatic loss for anyone. But in the same token, her mother had lived a long, fulfilling life. Her death certainly hadn't been a surprise. If anything, it had been a blessing. Maxine should have been able to look at it that way. She should have been willing to make her mother's funeral service a joyous celebration of a life lived well. Her mother had deserved nothing less. Just as Nell, today, had deserved nothing less.

It was an entirely different story if the death had been to a person in their prime. Or if the death had been sudden and tragic. If the death had occurred to a person who one could see had so much life left to live or so many more things to accomplish. Someone who was still needed desperately by others. Someone like Sharon and like Kyle.

With the clarity of the setting sun, Eric suddenly understood. He had been furious with Maxine. That's what had driven him to write that horrendous sermon afterwards. He'd been filled to overflowing with a righteous indignation.

How dare she have carried on like that? Was she some simpering sixty-year-old baby who could only feel loved by having people fawning all over her, offering her their sympathies? As he recalled, many had done just that too. And inside, he had sneered at each well-meaning gesture, calling them fools for falling victim to such selfish manipulations.

Why, he had held himself a stoic at Sharon and Kyle's funeral. No martyrdom for him. He did his crying in private, and he consoled others in public. That was his call—to minister to others and to build their faith. It wouldn't do to have people feeling sorry for him. That would only compromise his position.

That's also why Crow River had seemed the perfect place to move. No one knew him here. He'd offered only the vaguest sketch of the accident. Most people didn't even know that he'd had a son. There was always more sympathy when a child was taken. But here, he was free to start over, to concentrate on his ministry again.

Starting over, however, did *not* include a new wife. No one could ever replace Sharon, and he had no intention of settling for anything less. In fact, come to think of it, he had no intention whatsoever. He was happy with things just the way they were right now—peaceful and ordered.

This thought reminded Eric of Debra Culpepper. Perhaps he wasn't happy with *everything* as it was now. Debra, or any other woman for that matter, needed to understand that he simply wasn't interested in marrying again. But that presented a touchy problem. He certainly didn't want to hurt Debra's feelings. She was a sweet, sensitive person. She was loyal and conscientious. And her housekeeping skills were impeccable.

A knock on the open door intruded. He swiveled to see Kimberly framed in the doorway.

"Why are you sitting in the dark, Dad?"

"I was watching the sunset."

"It's dark now."

He glanced at the window. So it was. "I guess I got to thinking, and I lost track of time."

"Were you thinking about Mom and Kyle?"

"A little."

"Am I too big to sit on your lap?"

He pretended to size her up. "No. I think you'll still fit." She rounded the desk and settled down comfortably. "See? Perfect."

"Do you think about Mom and Kyle a lot?"

He slipped her hair behind her ear. "Every day."

"Me too."

He tucked her head in the crook of his neck and stroked her hair. She was his little Sharon. A real blessing.

"Sometimes," she continued, "I wonder why I'm still here."

Eric felt a lump in his throat. How often had he felt the same way? He swallowed. "You're still here, Kim, because God still has a reason for you to be."

"What?"

"I don't understand what you're asking."

"What reason does He have for me to be here? I mean...Kyle should be here then too. And Mom. I'm not a better person than them."

"None of us are better or worse, Kim. That isn't how God decides who should live and who should die."

"How does He decide then?"

"Oh honey. *That* is a very big question. None of us know how God decides that. If we did, I guess we wouldn't need Him."

Kim seemed satisfied with his answer. At least she settled more snugly against him. He wrapped his arms around her more securely and held her like that until her breathing deepened into the measured cadence of slumber. It was funny, he thought, how easily a child could accept God's superiority in matters like life and death. And he wondered again why it was so difficult for him.

Chapter 3

▼

"How'd you sleep last night, Mom?" Susan Justison had the phone receiver wedged between her ear and shoulder as she buttered her toast.

"Better than I thought after I had another good cry."

"Me too. It felt like I fell into a coma. Did you want me to come over today to help you with the thank you's?"

"No, dear. I don't think I'll get any further than sorting through the cards anyway. Besides, I know you deal better with stress when you're outdoors. And it's such a lovely day again today."

Susan glanced out her kitchen window. The sun had risen an hour earlier. Already the orb had turned from red to gold. The sky surrounding it was cloudless and iridescent blue. "It's perfect all right. If you're sure you don't need me, I was thinking of taking care of the parsonage windows today."

"Off with the storms and on with the screens again, huh? Why they didn't replace those old windows with combinations long ago, I'll never understand."

"Well, there's a lot of windows in that old house, Mom. It's a major project and adds up fast." It was a no brainer as far as Susan was concerned. Her services to switch the screens and storms twice a year were volunteered. All the church incurred was the cost of materials if repairs, replacements, or repainting were needed.

Her mother sighed. "Yes, I suppose. But if they ever *do* decide to modernize, they'd certainly better give the contract to you."

"I'm sure they will…if I'm the lowest bidder. That's really only right, you know. It's the congregation's money." Susan topped off her coffee. "Sorry to make this so short, Mom. But if you don't need me, I'd like to get an early start, and I've still gotta eat my breakfast and dress."

"I understand. Just be careful. I hate it when you're climbing ladders."

"I will. I always am. Love you."

"Love you too, Susan."

Two hours later, Susan was removing the first of the six upstairs storm windows. No one was home when she'd arrived, and she hadn't wanted to go inside without permission even though the door was unlocked. So she'd hauled the screen windows from the garage, swept and hosed them down to remove the winter dust and cobwebs, and had leaned them against each respective side where they'd be needed. By the time that was completed, Debra Culpepper had arrived to perform her daily housekeeping chores. Debra had greeted her warmly, expressed her sympathy over Nell, and let her inside to unfasten the catches that locked the windows in place.

Now she stood twelve feet above the ground on her aluminum extension ladder. The base was firmly anchored. The top rested securely against the overhead eave. She pulled a screwdriver from her tool belt and reached between the rungs to wedge it between the window and its frame. Working it in and out carefully at intervals of a few inches, she finally felt the window loosen like the top of a paint can when its seal has been breached. Susan double-checked the pulley that she'd attached to the ladder and the rope sling that she'd spread and tacked to the bottom of the frame. Assured that everything was in place, she reached around the ladder and levered the screwdriver a final time to fully release the window. Her outstretched hands caught each side securely at the same instant. Carefully, she lowered her burden into the sling and breathed a sigh of relief. One year she'd broken two windows due to her inattentiveness to the task.

Pulling her hammer from her belt, she again reached around and removed the nail on the left and on the right that secured the sling. The pulley rope was locked, and the weight of the window caused it to drop only an inch or so. With one hand, Susan held the window steady while she released the lock mechanism and maintained tautness on the rope with the other. In tandem, she eased out the rope as she descended the ladder a step at a time. Once her feet and cargo safely touched the ground, she smiled. Every year the first window was always the worst. After that the synchronization all came back to her.

By noon, Susan had replaced the storms with screens on all six of the upper windows. The ten on the lower level would go much faster since she could eliminate the ladder and pulley. She figured they'd only take her a couple more hours to do. But it was lunchtime, and that meant it was time to knock off and see how the guys were doing.

The Main Street Diner looked just the same as every weekday at lunchtime. A haze hovered at the ceiling in the front. White-uniformed waitresses sped efficiently between the closely placed tables and the raucous crowd that sat at them. The air smelled of deep fat fryer grease and cigarette smoke. It was nice that some things never changed. The same people were usually at their same table at the same time each day. Her own seat at the horseshoe lunch counter was waiting for her.

"Hi guys," she said as she sat down beside Marvin. Kevin and Andy were seated directly across from them as always.

"Hi Susie," Marvin said as he gave her his biggest smile. "Glad you could make it."

"I had to just to make sure you guys weren't playing hooky."

"Ahh," Marvin drawled with a wink. "I wouldn't dare do that this close to my retirement. I got a grandson I wanna live to play with, you know."

"Yeah. I figured I'd find *you* here. But those other two...," she began, raising her voice and directing a grin at Kevin and Andy, "I wasn't so sure about. They're a little wet behind the ears."

Kevin and Andy grinned. Both were in their twenties and married. Kevin had recently become a father. He defended them both. "We're not *that* wet. We know you'd give us shit if we didn't get the sheet-rocking finished."

"Sheet-rocking?" Susan tossed back, feigning seriousness. "Is *that* all you think you'll get done today?"

Andy, who was always slower to detect when she was teasing, said, "Well…yeah. What did you expect?"

She gave him a sober stare. "The sheet-rocking." She ticked the chore off on one finger. "The taping." She ticked off another. "*And* the sanding."

He reddened, catching on to her charade, and saluted. "Ai, Ai, Captain."

After their waitress had taken their orders, the conversation turned to Kevin's baby boy. He'd eaten cereal for the first time the night before and had needed a bath afterwards. Marvin related the time that his oldest had regurgitated his meal and they'd *both* needed a bath. Susan laughed merrily along with them. She really liked kids and got along with them pretty well. But she'd never had the overwhelming desire, like most women did, to have any of her own. She only regretted that her mother had been disappointed by her decision. Her mom had never said anything outright, but Susan knew that she'd once dreamed of grandchildren.

The truth of the matter was that Susan had dreams too, and she was living them now. She'd always loved hands-on projects. While other girls her age had been playing house, Susan had been alongside her dad learning how to build them.

Her dad had been a carpenter and even a plumber and an electrician in the days before you needed a special license to perform those trades. When they moved to California for a couple years before she was born, he'd dabbled in real estate. His gambles there had paid off, and he returned to Crow River with enough money to start a real estate agency. But his love for carpentry and home repair had never diminished. And he found that by combining his two interests, he ended up with a lucrative business. Ed's Realty invested in property that needed restoration and did exactly that—either reselling it afterwards or retaining it for rental purposes.

Susan was now the sole proprietor of her dad's company, and she loved getting up every morning. The four of them at the lunch counter performed the hands-on repair to the acquired property, as well as contracting their services to private homeowners. In her office she employed two full-time real estate agents. They sold property for clients or, with her approval, handled any acquisitions. She also employed two secretaries. Ed's Realty was going as strong as ever, and she knew that her dad in heaven was proud of her.

After lunch Susan bid her employees, who were also her friends, goodbye and picked up where she'd left off at the parsonage. When Debra departed later, she told Susan to feel free to go inside whenever she needed to do so. By three o'clock she was securing her extension ladder to the top of her company pickup when Pastor Masterson returned home.

"Hello, Susan," he greeted her. He glanced at the screened windows with appreciation. "Thank you. It'll be nice to be able to crack a window and get some of this fresh spring air inside."

"You're welcome." She smiled.

"I understand you do this every spring and fall. Seems like quite a chore for you, but the congregation and I certainly appreciate it. Frankly, I'm surprised you're all done already."

"Oh, I'm not *all* done. I need to caulk and repaint the storm windows yet so they'll be ready for fall. I hope you don't mind, but I put them in the other stall of the garage. I'll probably work on them over the next few weekday evenings."

"Fine…that's just fine." He turned again to survey the result of her efforts and nodded his head in satisfaction. "It's too bad the rest of your crew has already gone home. You all deserve some coffee."

She grinned. "Pastor, there was no crew. Just me."

His mouth dropped open. "But…how did you…and so quickly?"

"Hey, I've been doing this for years. Practice makes perfect."

He indicated the upstairs windows of which she always felt the most pride. "How could you—? Those windows must've been heavy."

She laughed. "Pastor, give me some coffee, and I'll put you out of your misery."

Just then a young girl walked up the drive, and Pastor Masterson introduced them. "Susan, this is my daughter, Kimberly. Kimberly, this is Susan Justison. Her mother is Evelyn. Susan took all of our storm windows off today and replaced them with screened windows. And she did it all by herself."

Kimberly was quiet and polite—not overly impressed with Susan's accomplishments of the day but that was understandable. Until you've stood twelve feet off the ground, holding an awkward and heavy window at arms length, and realized that you can't possibly peel yourself away from the ladder far enough to take a descending step…well, until then, you just couldn't understand.

A short while later, Susan had washed up, the coffee had perked, and the three of them were seated around the small table in the cozy kitchen. Sunny yellow curtains, no doubt a project of the church ladies' group, adorned the window, letting the light of a beautiful afternoon inside. Debra Culpepper must've baked the gingersnaps that Kimberly had placed on the china plate between them. Susan spread a paper napkin across her blue jeans and selected one that she placed before her on another napkin.

"Your mother and your aunt Nell were particularly close for sister-in-laws, weren't they?" Pastor asked.

"Yes. Extremely. They were friends since they were girls. Daddy was just Nell's older brother until he was stationed in Europe during World War II. Then he and my mother started writing each other."

"Ah…a wartime romance."

She nodded. "Ah huh. By the time he returned home, Mom says they looked at each other in an entirely different light."

"And your mother's lived in Crow River all her life then?"

Susan waited until she'd swallowed the piece of the marvelous molasses cookie she'd just nibbled off. "All except the two years when Dad had a bee in his bonnet to move West. They went to California then. Nell even went with."

"That's a bit unusual."

She shrugged. "Not really. Nell had nothing to tie her here, and she was always the adventurous sort." Susan glanced at the pastor and noticed his befuddled expression. She laughed. "Oh, heavens, she didn't *live* with them if that's what you're thinking. She took an apartment nearby."

He reddened. "I'm that transparent, huh?"

Susan sympathized with his embarrassment. Somehow it was odd to see a man looking a bit vulnerable. "I can see how you might've jumped to that conclusion. But no, I don't think that would've worked well at all. Mom and Nell may have been close, but their personalities were so different that...well, it wouldn't have worked at all. And Dad certainly wouldn't have put up with two women in the household."

He relaxed against the back of his chair, seeming to feel at ease again. "He must've learned how. When *you* came along, he became outnumbered."

She grinned with glee in her eyes. "Ah...that's because *I* had him wrapped around my finger." She turned to Kimberly who hadn't said a word, just sat quietly, eating her cookie daintily. "Kimberly, I'll bet *you* have your dad wrapped around your finger too, don't you?"

Kim blushed and smiled at him. "I...don't think so."

Her dad leaned closer to her, smiling fondly. "Of course you do, Kim. All little girls are the apple of their daddy's eyes."

Her smile broke so broadly that her whole face seemed to light up. Such a beautiful, well-mannered girl she was.

Soon the conversation turned to Susan's secret in dealing with the windows single-handedly. By this time, Kim had warmed to her and asked some very clever questions when she wanted clarification. "You see, Kim," Susan said in conclusion, "God didn't make us as strong as men, but He gave us something to make up for it."

"What?" she asked, by now hanging on Susan's every word.

Susan leaned back comfortably, satisfied that Kim had asked the magic question. "Ah," she said and sighed. "God gave us the brains." She tapped her head once for emphasis.

"Agh," Pastor groaned. "I could see that one coming a mile away. Traitor," he teased Kim, wagging his finger at her. "You played right into her trap."

Kim giggled.

"Oh but, Kim, it's absolutely true," Susan said with the utmost sincerity. "Why, do you know if it hadn't been for women, the very simplest of machines would've never been invented?"

Pastor shook his head with a smile. "Now *I* know how it feels to be outnumbered. Where are you going with this?"

She leaned closer, crooking her finger and inviting them to do the same. They complied. "Long, long ago in the days of the cave people, the men were responsible for bringing home the bacon…or the dinosaur meat. Their wives were to stay at home with their babies while they went away to the hunt. The men always did this in groups, you see, because there was safety in numbers. And they'd be gone for days and days."

"Who kept the women and babies safe from the dinosaurs while the men were gone?" Kim asked, wide-eyed with interest.

"Ah. That's where the problem came in. No one was left to protect the women but their own ingenuity which, fortunately, they had in abundance. The caves were wide open at the front, you see. Any wild animal that chose to could enter at will. The men of course, tried to convince them that this really wasn't much of a problem at all. Wild animals were afraid of fire. So all the women had to do to keep them out was to keep the home fires burning."

Pastor Masterson was again shaking his head and grinning.

"Well, in July, the women decided that they'd had enough. It was just too darn hot to keep a fire burning. So before their men left on the hunt, they begged and pleaded with them to simply roll the stone in front of the doorway. Caves, you see, had stones that could be rolled in place to close them up just like Jesus' tomb."

Kim nodded her understanding. Pastor raised a brow.

Susan sighed wearily. "But it was all to no avail. Wouldn't you know it, the men made some excuse about not having enough time and off they went on their merry way, carrying their spears. Well, the women were mighty ticked about that, let me tell you. So they all banned together to try to roll each stone into place. But they discovered that the stones had sat in their places for so many generations that they had sunk into a depression of their own making. 'Ah ha!' one of the women exclaimed. '*This* is why our men will not move the stones. They cannot budge them either.' So all the women went off to their homes to ponder day and night, all the while working tirelessly in the heat to keep their fires burning. And finally their efforts paid off, and they created one of the first simple machines to move their stones. Can you guess what it was, Kim?"

She shook her head.

"Pastor?" Susan turned a teacher's expression upon him.

He was rolling his eyes. "That would be the lever and the fulcrum," he stated dryly.

"Very, very good, Pastor," she teased.

Kim tapped her hand for attention. "But when the men came home, how did they get back in their caves?"

"Oh, alas. That's the shame of it. They couldn't."

"But weren't the women stuck inside then too?"

"Kimberly," she chastised. "Women always think ahead."

"Knowing Susan here," Pastor interjected, "the women had probably already tunneled to a back door that their men knew nothing about."

"Heavens no!" Susan exclaimed, fanning herself. "Such a sweaty proposition they would've never attempted. No, they had taken the time beforehand to measure their stones. And when they were in place, each left just enough room for them and the children to crawl over the top."

"Let me guess." Pastor laughed once with glee. "The men were too big to fit through, right?"

"Bingo. There's hope for your kind yet."

Chapter 4

▼

Evelyn Justison's alarm awoke her before 6:00 a.m. as it did every other weekday morning. Her first thought was that it was Friday—the day that she did her dusting and vacuuming. Maybe she'd stop and visit Nell in the afternoon. Then, with a start, she remembered that Nell was gone. Memories of the funeral came flooding back. And quickly on its heels, came the recollection of the overwhelming box of sympathy cards for which thank you's needed to be addressed. At least it would keep her busy, give her something constructive to accomplish.

She stiffly slipped out of bed and made her way across the hall to the bathroom. As she splashed cold water on her face, she laughed sarcastically. "Oh Evelyn, it's a sad state of affairs when you relish the idea of writing out thank you cards." When had life become so dull and unfulfilling? But she knew the answer. It had gradually happened after Edward had died five years before.

Her life had never been as exciting as Nell's, but it had been satisfying until then. After all, there was nothing Evelyn had ever wanted more than a husband and then a family. The husband had come almost effortlessly. She'd known Edward was the one as soon as they'd started exchanging letters. Until then, he had only been Nell's older brother—the young boy who'd teased them and then the young man who'd moved away and later joined the service. But a funny thing happens to a man in a war. Faced with the very real issues of life and death, Edward became very philosophical, though he never really lost the sense of humor she'd always admired. And he also became very romantic. Evelyn smiled wistfully as she moved back to her room to dress.

The family had come with far more effort and despair. In those days one didn't consult a doctor when a child couldn't be conceived. There were no doctors to consult for such a thing. Or if there were, neither Evelyn nor Edward would have done so anyway. They believed they'd have a child if God willed it. And finally after nine years, God answered their prayers with the miracle that was Susan.

While Susan had been growing up, Evelyn had never known such joy and fulfillment. Scraped knees and disappointments were hers to soothe. Achievements were hers to cheer. It had been quite an adjustment when Susan had left for four years to attend college. But she'd come home every summer to work with Edward. And of course, she'd settled here afterwards. Evelyn was content with the way things had worked out.

But after Edward had died, Evelyn felt as though she no longer fit in anywhere. There was no one for whom to do things. No one to welcome home at night. No one with whom to share her deepest thoughts. Life was lonely, and life was too long. Why did God keep people around who had outlived their usefulness?

While Evelyn set the coffee to perking, she remembered with dismay her promise to Hattie Carlson. Why today, of all days, had she agreed to go to the nursing home? She was feeling depressed enough as it was. Then she laughed aloud, recalling that *agreement* had little to do with the decision. Hattie had railroaded her.

That afternoon when she walked through the home's glazed double doors, Evelyn was immediately assailed by the scent of sickness and death. Or was it the prevailing pallor of hopelessness that she sensed? Or perhaps it was simply urine and aging bodies. Whatever it was, it confirmed the opinion she'd always held. She hated the home.

Hattie was in her room—one that she shared with a small, shriveled woman who was sleeping in the first bed. Hattie was seated in her motorized wheelchair, facing the window, and peering out at the children at recess in the schoolyard across the street.

Evelyn came further into the room and asked quietly, "Hattie? Am I disturbing you?"

The wheelchair whirled to face her with surprising speed. Hattie clutched her sweater together at her neck. The green eyes in her weathered face lit with pleasure at seeing her. "Good heavens no, Evie. I've been expecting you."

"I'm sorry that I'm a little late. I was addressing thank you's and...well, the time ran away from me."

"I figured as much. That can be a depressing task. Glad I could save you from it."

Evelyn laughed. She couldn't help it. The irony was ridiculous. Hattie stared up quizzically. Before Evelyn could check herself, she was explaining aloud. "Addressing thank you's was far less depressing than this place." She gasped and brought her hand to her mouth. "Oh, I'm sorry, Hattie. I didn't mean that to sound so...so—"

"Insulting?"

She blushed and glanced away. "Yes."

"Agh." Hattie waved her hand, indicating the guest chair beside her. "It's nothin' I haven't heard before. Sit a spell." Evelyn did. "Livin' here's really no more depressing than livin' in your own home might sometimes seem to you. Don't you get lonely from time to time?"

Hattie's flashing green eyes stared into hers, demanding honesty. Evelyn sighed heavily. "More often than not."

"It's no different here. I went through a time when I was down more than up. And as much as I despised myself for it, I just couldn't seem to look on the bright side of things. To tell you the truth, it had me just plain stumped."

Evelyn couldn't imagine why. One only had to look at the comatose roommate, hear the occasional moans that carried down the hall, or smell the sickening stench to understand why Hattie's adjustment had been so difficult. "Why were you stumped?"

She shook her head. "'Cause it just wasn't like me a'tall. You probably don't know it, but my life has been one tragedy after another. But I never looked at it that way. I concentrated on the blessings instead and could always find more of them than anything else."

"That's a wonderful gift."

"Yes it is. That's exactly what it is...a gift. So I asked myself why that gift had deserted me when I first moved in here."

"It's a depressing place. A person only has to step through the door to realize that you're surrounded by death. I think a saint would have trouble ignoring that."

Hattie guffawed. "Lord, Evelyn. Don't ever make the mistake of placing me in *that* category." She slapped her knee. "Nosiree. A saint I am not."

She smiled good-naturedly in response to the devilish twinkle in Hattie's eyes. "So how did you rise above your circumstances here?"

"It's not a pretty story, I'm afraid. At first I blamed everyone else. Oh, not to their face, mind you. No, I was certainly more clever than that. But inside, I'd find myself shaking my head at all the people around me who'd just given up on life. How dare they give up? I thought. It ain't over 'till it's over. We've all got our places here until that happens."

Evelyn leaned closer, intrigued. Hadn't this been just the idea she'd been contemplating this morning? Why was she still here when she'd outlived her usefulness? "Did you realize that life isn't fulfilling unless you have purpose?" That's what Evelyn had concluded.

"Heck no. I realized *that* a long time ago. I've got purpose...known what it is for a long time now."

Evelyn raised a quizzical brow.

"I'm here to build people up. Person goes through the stuff I have so they know how it feels to be in another's shoes. That's my gift. That's my purpose. But all of a sudden I landed here, and I realized that I was angry at God about it. Do you know why?" Her eyes bored into Evelyn's, who shook her head. "Most of these people don't *want* to be built up. They'd rather wallow around in self-pity. 'Course some of 'em's senile. I don't mean them. I mean the ones who still got their mind and choose not to count their blessings."

"That can be a hard thing for most people, Hattie. Remember, that's *your* gift. You may have been expecting something that they just couldn't do."

"Ah you're a smart one, Evie." She beamed a smile of admiration. "That's exactly what I finally figured out. But the question still remained, 'Why did God put me here, of all places, with people who could've cared less?' And I'm afraid that while I was tryin' to figure all that out, I started acting up a bit."

"Acting up?"

"Oh, you know me. I got a devilish streak a mile long. I love practical jokes. Just can't seem to keep 'em in sometimes."

"I see."

"Yes. Well, I started out with little things, you know?" She pointed to the slumbering form in the neighboring bed. "The nurse would come in to help Adeline there to the bathroom. I'd wheel the medication cart to the next doorway. Little stuff like that. They'd'a never caught on neither if I hadn't gotten a terribly wicked idea one day. I just couldn't help it."

Evelyn raised a brow.

"Just look at Addie there." Hattie pointed again to her roommate who lay practically unconscious, mouth hanging open, small snores escaping. "She's ninety-three, sleeps all day, mind's kinda gone. I didn't think there'd really be much harm in finding out."

"Finding out what?"

"What she'd look like with a drinking straw stuck up each nostril."

Evelyn studied Adeline seriously for several moments. What a humiliating thing to have done to the poor woman. Good heavens, Hattie was a character. No wonder her and Nell had hit it off so well. Just then Adeline emitted a short series of soft snorts. Her nose twitched. Drool slid from the corner of her gaping mouth. Unbidden, an image formed in Evelyn's mind—two straws protruding from the woman's nose. The vision was so hilarious that she couldn't contain a giggle. She caught Hattie's gleam of pride and grasped how ridiculous the whole situation must've been. What kind of elderly woman wheeled around, sticking drinking straws up the noses of helpless residents in a nursing home? Evelyn's stomach ached, tears of laughter escaped from her eyes, and still she couldn't will herself to stop. She wondered if Hattie had a stash of stolen straws hidden somewhere—enough to infest the noses of the entire population.

"Evie, honey." Hattie slapped her back. "You gotta get a hold of yourself. Even *I* didn't laugh that hard." She handed Evelyn a tissue.

Grabbing it, she held it to her eyes. Evelyn made several attempts to speak before she finally succeeded. "D...Do you mean you've discovered that your purpose here is to torture the rest of the populace?"

Hattie guffawed. "Heck no. Any prankster worth their salt will tell you there's no satisfaction playin' a joke on someone who doesn't even know they've been had. No, it's the employees here who've been cheered by my presence. Why, they've even given me a pet name that I'm pretty proud of."

Before Evelyn could ask what that might be, a nurse planted her feet in the open doorway. Her arms were stubbornly crossed at her chest. Her eyes bore into those belonging to the occupant of the wheelchair. "Hattie from Hades," she barked in an accusatory tone. "Are you the thief responsible for stealing a box of latex surgical gloves from the storeroom?"

The expression of the accused was wide-eyed innocence as she shook her head. "Wish I'd thought of it though," she admitted. "A gal could have a lot of fun with those."

"Yeah, I'll just bet you could." The nurse's eyes sparkled. She turned her gaze to Evelyn. "*Please* tell me that you're here to spring her for a few hours."

"Ah...well...no—"

"It's okay, Evie. Maybe you and I can plan a little getaway after all those thank you's are done, huh?"

"Ah...oh...certainly. Yes, we might be able to arrange something sometime."

It wasn't until Evelyn was on her way home that she realized she'd been railroaded again. Funny though. It didn't really bother her. In fact, she found herself looking forward to an outing with Hattie. She really did have a gift for building people up.

Oh, how Evelyn wished that she was a bit more like that—outgoing and fun loving. Life would certainly be more exciting and entertaining. She sighed dismissively. But that just wasn't her way. Everyone was different. She accepted that.

The phone rang shortly after she'd entered her house. She caught it in the kitchen by the third ring. "Hello?"

"Mom? How's it going?"

"Fine, Susan. I just got back from the nursing home."

"Oh, that's right. I forgot that you were going over to visit Hattie today."

"Were you looking for me for something, dear?"

"Um...I just wanted to let you know that you don't need to worry about going through Nell's apartment on top of everything else."

Evelyn sat down on the kitchen chair. She'd hardly given a thought to that. But of course, Susan would need to get the place readied for another tenant sometime soon. "How soon would you need me to then?"

"Don't worry about it at all, Mom. I can take care of that chore for you. I cleaned out the refrigerator this afternoon. A few more evenings toward the end of next week should take care of the rest. You know, now I'm real glad that Nell sold that big old house, had that auction—"

"No, Susan. Absolutely not. You will *not* go through Nell's things. That's *my* job."

Silence greeted her outburst.

Evelyn inhaled a calming breath. "Are you still there, honey?"

"Yeah." Susan sighed. "Wow. I'm sorry, Mom. I didn't know you felt so strongly about it. I mean…I only suggested it to help you out."

"Of course." Evelyn felt sick with regret. She'd overreacted terribly. "I understand that, dear. I appreciate it. You're a wonderful, thoughtful daughter. It's just that I'd like to be the one to sort through all the memories…by myself, if you can understand that."

"Sure. I know how close you and Aunt Nell were."

"Did you have a timeframe, dear? When would you like to have the apartment vacated?"

"Not really. I was thinking that the end of the month might be nice, but it's not necessary. Take your time, Mom."

"Thank you, sweetheart. I'll try to get it done by then."

Two weeks, Evelyn thought as she replaced the receiver. Two weeks to sort through all of Nell's personal belongings. Two weeks to locate Nell's diary. That should be plenty of time. Thank God Susan had agreed so readily to allow her to do it alone. There were some things that Susan just didn't need to know. Knowledge that was better buried along with Nell.

Chapter 5

"How are you doing this fine Saturday morning, Pastor Masterson?"

At the familiar voice of his friend, Eric glanced over and smiled. "Not too bad, Father Marcus."

Together, they exited the country club where the monthly breakfast meeting of the Crow River Ministerial Association had just adjourned. It was a common greeting that they bestowed upon each other. It accentuated the ecumenical feeling that their mutual friendship inspired. Ten years ago, it just wouldn't have done for a Catholic priest and a Lutheran minister to associate so openly. But they had far more in common than not. Both were in their early forties. Both enjoyed a fitness regimen that included a morning jog. Both shared a devotion to God and to their parishioners. And of course, both were single.

"Sorry to hear you had another funeral to conduct this week." The priest's brown hair was wavy and lent him a boyish appearance, despite the sprouting silver strands. His brown eyes were sincere.

"Yeah. Nell Justison. But it wasn't too bad at all, kind of a festive occasion really."

"Those are the best. It'd be nice if they could all be that way."

"Amen."

"So what happened to you this morning?"

Eric knew he was referring to his absence from their punctual run around Round Lake. "I overslept."

Marcus stopped dead in his long stride, halting Eric with a hand on his arm. "You what? Did I hear you right? Mister Up-Before-the-Sunrise overslept?"

He shrugged. "I...ah...stayed up late wrapping up Sunday's sermon."

"So?"

"What do you mean *so*?"

"So," he stressed, "you're not spilling it all."

"Why would you think that?"

"'Cause you're not making eye contact, buddy. The only time you don't do that is when you're holding something back."

Man, this guy knew him too well. Eric realized that he might've felt uncomfortable if that fact wasn't a two-way street. He knew Marcus just as well. "Okay. I had trouble falling asleep. Then I woke up in the middle of the night too. I probably slept a total of three hours tops."

"Why, Eric? What's bothering you?"

They'd resumed walking and had reached their cars. Eric sighed with his hand on the door handle. "It's Debra Culpepper."

They shared a significant look over the roof of his Taurus. Marcus shrugged. "I can't say I'm surprised. A bit envious maybe, but not surprised."

"Envious? You *like* her?"

"You *don't*?"

"Well, yes. She's a nice person, but I don't like her like *that*."

Marcus held upended hands in a gesture of surrender. "Neither do I. That's not what I meant."

"Then what are you envious of?"

"Sheesh, Eric. I'm only envious that for you such a thing is a real possibility. For me, it's not."

Eric had never really considered what that might be like. Surely he knew, intellectually, what the vows of a priest entailed. But he'd never known one as a friend so well before. He'd never actually allowed himself to consider one as a fellow human being with all the needs and temptations that this presented. He suddenly felt chagrined at his own shallowness and insensitivity. Why, of all people, had he brought up such a subject with Marcus? But he knew the answer as soon as he'd asked it. He didn't think of Marcus as a priest but as a friend, probably the closest one he'd ever had. "I'm sorry, man."

"Hey. No need to feel ashamed, Eric. I'm kind of flattered that you'd bring it up. It tells me you can look beyond this collar that I wear. Even a priest needs a good friend, you know."

They smiled at each other. "Well, friend, can I get your opinion about the whole thing then?"

Marcus sobered. "I'd be honored."

"Okay. Let's head over to my place and talk."

A short while later, Marcus gave a long, low whistle as he surveyed the fully stocked and orderly pantry. "Yep. She's got it for you all right."

"So what am I supposed to do?"

"You really don't like her?" He caught Eric's look of frustration. "I mean…like *that*? 'Cause you know, this room here is the epitome of domesticity."

"I know. She'd make someone a wonderful wife. But not me. I have no interest in her or anyone else. I'll never marry again."

"Never say *never*."

Eric led the way back through the doorway and resumed his seat at the table. Marcus gave him a long look before doing the same.

"Okay. So you don't want to marry again. I can accept that. I don't mind saying that I don't understand it, but I can see that you mean it. So you're wondering how you can get that point across without hurting her feelings, right?"

"Exactly." Eric rubbed his temples.

Marcus sighed. "That's a tough one. But I'd say you should just level with her. Shoot straight, with as much honesty and compassion as you possess."

"I'd already figured that out during the long night, but how do I even begin?"

His friend opened his mouth to respond, then stopped himself as Kim entered the kitchen from the dining room. He beamed her a smile. "Hi there, Kim."

She beamed back. "Hi, Father Marcus. How are you?"

"Not too shabby. How's it goin' in school for you?"

"Good. I like it. I'm already dreading summer."

Marcus cast a confused expression Eric's way before responding. "Why would you be dreading summer?"

She shrugged. "The days will get long. I won't know what to do with myself."

"You could get a job."

"I'm only thirteen."

"Couldn't you babysit or something?"

She leaned against the door jam. "Yeah. I suppose. But I don't know anyone who needs a sitter."

Eric vaguely sensed that Marcus was watching him. He hated to admit that he'd hardly been paying any attention to their conversation. He was trying to figure out how he could approach Debra concerning the subject they'd been discussing before Kim had intruded. What was he supposed to say? "Look, Debra. I can tell that you have expectations that I just can't meet." No, that was lame. Wouldn't any self-respecting person deny that that was the case? Then he'd look stupid for even bringing up such a thing.

"Looks like your dad could use a sitter, Kim." The two of them laughed. "He's in a world of his own. Needs some direction." Suddenly Marcus was tapping his arm excitedly. "Eric, that's it!"

"Huh?"

"Kim can spend the summer doing Miss Culpepper's job. She'll keep busy. You can pay her. It'll be perfect!"

Eric focused on his friend's animated face as the words sunk in. Perfect! It wasn't the whole solution, but it was a good start.

Kimberly seemed happy with the prospect of a summer with a constructive pastime that would also earn her some cash. After she returned to her room, the two of them resumed their conversation in a different vein.

"You were a boy scout." Marcus posed the sentence as a statement, rather than a question.

Eric blushed. "Eagle."

"Figures. But I didn't mean that literally. I meant you were one of those saintly boys."

"Weren't you?"

Marcus laughed. "Hardly."

"What were you then?"

"Me?" He pointed at himself. "I was the black sheep."

"You're kidding!" Eric was incredulous.

"Hey." His friend shrugged. "God works miracles."

"I guess. Gee. I never would've guessed that. But...how did you know I wasn't?"

"Sheesh! It's obvious. You're so...so—"

"What?" Eric felt defensive.

"Well, don't get mad. I was complimenting you. I was just trying to think of the best word."

"Which is?"

"You're so concerned about everyone else's feelings."

"And that's good?"

"Heck, yeah. But you've got to consider your own too, you know."

"What do you mean by that?"

Marcus studied him for a while. "Nothing," he finally responded. "I'd better be heading home. I'm kind of tired." He grinned. "After all, I *ran* today."

"Yeah, yeah, rub it in."

"Well, you know, I don't have all the *women* problems that you have."

"Yeah, yeah. Cut it out." Suddenly Kimberly burst excitedly into the room again, obviously on a mission. "What's up, honey?"

"Susan's here. I'm going to go out to the garage to see her." She was already to the porch before she completed her explanation.

Marcus raised a brow. "Susan Justison? Don't tell me that you really have another woman giving you problems."

"Nah. She's just caulking the storms in the garage during her free time."

"Ah. She's still taking care of that, huh?"

"Yep. She's quite the handy woman."

"You can say that again. She puts some guys to shame. They don't work much harder than her."

"Yes. I get the impression she doesn't appreciate chauvinistic males."

"No room for them in her world. That's probably why she never got married."

"Could be. I was wondering about that."

"About what?"

Eric chose his words carefully. Marcus was bound to take this the wrong way. "Oh, nothing. I was just curious myself why she'd never gotten married."

As he'd suspected, Marcus raised a quizzical brow. But Eric was literally saved by the bell as the phone shrilled. He stood and plucked the receiver off the wall. "Pastor Masterson."

His brother's voice greeted him. "Eric?"

"What's up, John?" He called from Chicago about once a month, but he sounded unusually desperate today.

"I'd like to come for a visit if you've got the space."

"Sure. That's great. Marcy and the kids too?"

"Ah...no. No, they won't be coming."

"John, what's wrong? You sound...I don't know...weird."

"Well, I feel weird. Marcy's kicked me out."

"What did you do?"

A lengthy silence followed Eric's question. "I'm sorry," his brother finally said. "I shouldn't have called you. Hey, forget it. You don't need this. I'm sure you've got problems of your own."

"No." Eric spoke quickly, afraid that John would hang up, regretting that his question had sounded like an accusation. "You're always welcome here, John. You know that. To tell you the truth, I'd appreciate the company."

His brother sighed. "Are you sure?"

"Positive." Eric held his breath, awaiting John's response.

"Okay. I'm flying in to Minneapolis next Saturday."

"What flight? I'll pick you up."

"No need. I'm renting a car. Just give me some directions to your new place."

Eric did so, then hung up the phone slowly. His mind was spinning with the possibilities, wondering why his sister-in-law had given his brother the boot.

"Problems?" His friend's voice intruded.

"Ah...possibly." He wearily turned and met Marcus' concerned gaze. "It seems my brother's having some marital problems."

"I'm really sorry to hear that." His eyes showed his sincerity.

"Thanks. Me too." Eric sat down heavily.

"Younger?" To Eric's confused expression, he added, "Brother. Is John your younger brother?"

"Yeah. And only."

"That's tough. I'm guessing he wasn't the boy scout."

Eric grimaced. "That obvious, huh?" He slapped his fist into his open palm. "I keep doing that, you know? Opening my mouth and hurling out accusations at him without thinking."

Marcus leaned closer, inviting and holding eye contact. "What are you talking about?"

"Well, you heard me. 'What did you do?' That's the first thing I asked him when he told me."

"So what?"

"So what?" He straightened defiantly. "That's *exactly* the kind of reaction they lectured us about in seminary. 'Listen,' they said. 'Think before you speak. Never, ever sound judgmental.'"

"Sounds like excellent advice. Not practical at all times, but certainly excellent advice."

"Of course it's excellent advice. It's St. James through and through. Chapter three, verse five. 'Likewise the tongue is a small part of the body, but it makes great boasts. Consider what a great forest is set on fire by a small spark.'" He leaned back in defeat. "I blew it again."

"Yep. Like I said, *so what?*" He shooed Eric's planned protest with a wave of his hand. "St. James also says in verse two, 'We all stumble in many ways. If anyone is never at fault in what he says, he is a perfect man, able to keep his whole body in check.'"

Eric was both angry and impressed. Their biblical battles were sometimes fierce, and he hated to lose. "And your point is?"

"You're human, Eric. To err is human."

"That's not biblical."

"So what? It's philosophical. Are you going to start disallowing philosophy now?"

"No. It's allowed…as long as it's biblically based…and…well, don't get carried away with it."

"Yes, master." Marcus bowed his head in a mock gesture of reverence to his opponent.

Eric punched his arm.

"Ouch! What was that for?"

He grinned. "The Bible says, 'Thou shalt have no other gods before me.' You're acting blasphemous."

"Give me a break. I'm horsing around."

"I know."

"Yeah? Well, give yourself a break once in a while too, Eric. I'm not saying it's not good to try to be perfect. But you've got to remember that it's an impossible goal. You're going to mess up every day. That's just the way it is. That's human. God even expects it."

Eric knew the truth of his words. What a fine line we walk between arrogant perfection and justified humility. What a tough battle we are called to wage every single day of our lives. Sometimes life seemed too long. He glanced up to see that Marcus' face held an expectant expression.

"So?" his friend asked.

"So what?"

"Did I win that round?"

Eric punched his arm again.

Chapter 6

"Ohh," Kim moaned in frustration. "You make it look so easy."

"You're doing just fine," Susan encouraged. "Just keep even pressure on your trigger finger." Kim shifted her grip on the caulking gun and made another attempt to lay a straight bead. It was bumpy, as Susan had expected, but fixable.

"But it's so squiggly."

"No problem. I'll show you how to smooth it out when you've finished that side."

Kim reached the end, heaved a sigh of relief, and set the gun aside.

Susan licked her index finger and ran it along the bead. "See. It looks just like a pro did it. Piece a cake." She'd scraped the paint and putty from five of the storm windows the evening before. Her goal for the afternoon was the caulking. Having Kim join her had been a pleasant surprise. She appreciated the company.

"I don't know," Kim said doubtfully. "It takes me so long. Maybe I could scrape some of the others for you."

"Nope. Can't do that. It'll raise all kinds of dust, and paint chips will be flying all over. Can't have them landing on the wet putty."

"Training a little protégé?" The priest's voice came from the open garage doorway.

Susan glanced up to see him standing there, watching them and smiling. "Heaven forbid, Father Marcus. This town isn't big enough for two of me."

"Amen to that. So I can breathe a sigh of relief then?" He grinned.

"By all means. Breathe on."

Kim's father joined him. "Kimmy? I'm going to go over to the church office to get some work done. Probably won't be home until about five."

"Okay, Dad. Look. I laid a straight bead."

He stepped inside to survey the storm window to which she excitedly pointed. "Wow. That's pretty good, honey. So you're helping Susan, huh?"

She nodded. "Sorta. It's kind of fun."

"Just make sure you're not bugging her, okay?" He ruffled her hair.

"She's not at all," Susan assured him. "I appreciate her company."

"Good, good. Then I won't have to worry about her being bored while I'm gone."

"Nope. I'll keep her busy."

The two men departed, walking together to their cars. After a few more words to each other, Father Marcus patted the pastor on the back in farewell and they each drove away.

Kim enthusiastically worked beside her for three more hours. The caulking went so quickly that Kim talked her into scraping a few more windows after all. The afternoon was so mild and sunny that they carried each one to the concrete patio slab. When Susan decided that they'd done enough for the day, she put her tools away while Kim swept up the mess they'd created.

"Do you ever do any girl things?" Kim asked.

Susan laughed. "What do you mean, *girl* things?"

Kim shrugged. "Oh, you know...cooking, cleaning."

"Sure. I have to eat, so I cook. I own a house, so I clean. Actually, I like doing both."

"Could you teach me?"

The girl's face looked so hopeful and desperate all at the same time. Susan was stabbed by the thought that she was motherless. "I'd be happy to, Kim. But maybe you should ask Miss Culpepper first. I mean, she might feel bad if you don't, being she's already doing your housekeeping."

"That might be awkward."

Susan almost laughed at the grown up tone of her voice. She was so serious and mature for a thirteen-year-old. The thought occurred to her that it must be a bit stifling being the minister's daughter. "Why would it be awkward?"

"I think my dad plans to dismiss her."

"Dismiss her? But why?"

She shrugged. "Maybe because of me. He and Father Marcus were just talking about me getting a job this summer so I'll have something to keep me busy and to earn some money. They thought it would be perfect if I took over Miss Culpepper's chores."

"I see." Susan thought that was a bit odd since Debra Culpepper was noted for her perfectionism and thoroughness. Apparently though, Kim's father felt that Kim's needs were more important. She certainly couldn't fault him for that. "When did you want to start learning a few things?"

Kim blushed and stared down at her tennis shoes. "W...would you have any time today?" She glanced up and hastily added, "I mean, I thought it'd be nice to make a nice dinner. It's Miss Culpepper's day off and, well...all she left was oyster hotdish again. Dad just puts that down the garbage disposal." She gasped and covered her mouth. "Oh! I wasn't supposed to tell anyone that."

Susan laughed. So *that* was the way of it, she thought. Debra Culpepper had deemed the pastor worthy of her famous hotdish. "Don't worry about me. My lips are sealed." They both grinned. "Let's get cleaned up, and we'll begin cooking lesson number one."

An hour later, the house was fragrant with the aroma of meatloaf baking in the oven and steamy with the scent of potatoes and carrots cooking on the stove. "All you have left to do now, Kim, is to—"

"I know, I know. Set the table, start the gravy, turn off the vegetables, and take the meatloaf out of the oven."

"At what time?"

"Five o'clock."

"Right. And remember to—"

"Turn off the burners and the oven."

"Right again. You're a fast learner, kid."

Kim beamed a proud smile.

"Now don't let that go to your head. You have to do all the cleanup too, and *that* is *not* a fun chore."

"Dad will help me with that." She stated it matter-of-factly, no doubt in her mind.

"Really," Susan replied dryly. "Well, good for him. Not many guys bother to get their hands in dishwater, and they don't know what to do with a dishtowel."

"Dad's always helped me."

"Uh huh." Susan turned the burner under the carrots down to *warm*. "But I'll bet he never helped your mother." She regretted the words the instant she'd spoken them. How callous could she be? But a glance at Kim revealed that the girl didn't seem to be offended, only thoughtful.

"You know, you're right. I don't remember him helping Mom in the kitchen." She perched a finger on her chin. "I wonder why not?"

"It's considered *women's* work, that's why. Guys don't like to bother themselves with that. They figure it's their wife's job."

"You sound kind of mad about it."

Susan checked herself. Had her sarcasm gotten the better of her again? Way to go, she chided herself. Preaching your rhetoric to the minister's daughter. "I didn't mean to sound angry, Kim. I've just seen it happen that way for a lot of my friends. Guys slip a ring on their finger, and then they think they've got themselves a live-in slave." Ouch, she thought. Nothing like going from bad to worse. Maybe she should just quit while she was behind before she dug herself a bigger hole.

"Is that why you never got married?"

The question hung in the air while Susan digested it. Finally she responded in a surprised tone. "I think you've hit the nail on the head. I've just never seen myself as fitting into the housewife mold."

"But don't you get lonely?"

"Nope. Got a dog." And the cat kept her warm at night, she added silently. What more did an independent woman need? It had been good enough for Aunt Nell. It was good enough for Susan.

"Thanks for teaching me," Kim told her later as she prepared to leave.

"No problem. You just pick your dad's brain for some other things he likes to eat, and I'll teach you how to make something else next week." With her hand on the doorknob, she had another thought. "Oh, and there's no reason to tell your dad that you had help, okay? Besides, you did everything yourself anyway. All I did was supervise."

A few minutes later, Susan parked her pickup diagonally in the lot of the Crow River supermarket. She checked her watch as she got out. Five o'clock. She wondered briefly if Kim had remembered to take the meatloaf out, but then realized there was no need to worry. If anyone was responsible, it was that kid.

Grabbing a cart once she'd cleared the automatic door, she aimed it down the produce aisle. Tomatoes, broccoli, cauliflower. She selected the freshest of each product and gently placed them in the cart. Her mother had once chided her for not growing a garden. But who had the time? Potatoes she had at home in abundance, so she passed them by and headed up the pasta and sauce aisle. Unbidden, the image of the parsonage pantry came to mind. She smiled and almost laughed out loud. So Debra Culpepper had her sights set on the preacher. And obviously he wanted nothing to do with it, judging by his plan to replace her with Kim. Lord, help him. He'd need a better idea than that if he hoped to escape her clutches. There was one desperate woman.

"Susan, how are you?"

She glanced up to see Cindy Gunderson, a former classmate, dead ahead. Shit, she thought. Her own fault for being so inattentive. It wasn't that she disliked Cindy. In fact, she was a very sincere person. But it was that very sincerity that always made Susan feel uncomfortable…small in some way…as though Cindy felt pity for her. "I'm just fine, Cindy." She smiled. "Thanks for asking."

"I was *so* sorry to hear about Nell. How are you and your mom doing?"

"We're getting along. It was a shock, you know, but a person manages."

"Yeah." She nodded. "A day at a time. That's all you can do."

"I hear you have a wedding coming up in your family in June."

Cindy's face beamed proudly. "Yeah. Cheryl. The first one." Rolling her shoulders, she said, "Wow," on a long exhalation. "It's a *lot* of work and a *lot* of expense, but it's pretty exciting."

"I'm sure it is. And I'm sure everything will go just fine too. You always were a great organizer."

"Thanks."

There was that sincere smile again. No pity, though. Susan wondered if she'd been reading Cindy wrong all these years. Or maybe enough years had passed that Cindy had finally realized there was no need to pity her. That would be great. Brief glimpses of their childhood antics flashed through Susan's mind. They'd been such good friends, swearing they'd still be sleeping over at each other's homes when they were eighty. Now *that* would be weird under the present circumstances.

"What?" Cindy was asking.

"Huh?" Susan brought herself back to the conversation.

"You were shaking your head."

"Was I?" Susan blushed. "Sorry. Guess my mind's wandering."

Cindy looked guilty, as though she'd been reading her thoughts. "Well, I'm sure you have a lot going on too. I should let you get back to your shopping."

Susan nodded, suddenly feeling awkward. "Hey, it was nice talking to you, Cindy." She pushed her cart forward but stopped when they were abreast and held Cindy's gaze. "I mean that."

A bright smile greeted her statement and eyes that seemed washed with relief. "Thanks, Susan."

By six o'clock Susan was turning down Oak Street. The stately trees, for which the street was named, draped an unending arch overhead. Smattered warmth and sunshine danced on the pavement to the slow sway of their branches. They looked like spring green lace in the gentle evening breeze. Elms and maples were far ahead in the density of their foliage, but oaks always had the last laugh in autumn, clinging tenaciously to their leaves.

Susan's elegant Victorian waited patiently on the corner where Oak Street yielded to the cemetery. Few people preferred that their first view each morning be that of a graveyard, but Susan didn't mind. It was peaceful. And the abundance of birds guaranteed the sweetest chorus of nature on all but the hottest days of summer. Besides, she'd gotten her haven for a song. The house had been dilapidated and lonely and only too ready for her loving restoration.

She backed her pickup in the driveway and halted in front of the attached garage. Excited, but muffled, barking greeted her as she debarked. Its source—a slate colored schnauzer, sporting a beard and moustache and topped with perky ears—was framed in the lower half of the breezeway window. She opened the door and caught the furry bundle as Peanut leapt from the window seat and into her arms. Wiggling intensely, he lavished her neck with sloppy laps. "Okay, okay," she said with a smile. "That's enough. I missed you too, boy."

Depositing his squirmy body on the floor, she opened the inner door and stepped into the kitchen. Owlish green eyes watched her unblinkingly from the top of the refrigerator where her feline perched regally. "And how are you, Princess?" The cat gracefully arched and dropped soundlessly to the floor. Princess orbited Susan's ankles, where she deposited a generous portion of her fur.

After filling her pets' dishes and luring them out from underfoot, Susan hauled in her groceries and put them away. She prepared a spring garden salad and reheated a portion of wild rice and a chicken breast in the microwave. By the time she sat down at the table to eat her fare, Peanut and Princess had already consumed their own. They sat expectantly, one on each side of her chair.

"So what do you guys want to do tonight, huh?" She forked a piece of moist chicken into her mouth, chewed, savored, and swallowed. "How about a walk? Peanut, you'd like a walk, wouldn't you?"

The dog sat tensely on his haunches, tongue lolling and eyes pleading.

She turned to the cat that also sat on her haunches, but had managed the appearance of aloofness even while her owlish eyes drilled into Susan's. "How about you, Princess? I'll bet you'd rather curl up on the couch with me, wouldn't you?"

The cat emitted a short mewl.

The dog retracted his tongue for a moment, then let it slide out the other side. His stare slipped from Susan's face to her plate and back to her face again.

"You guys already ate your dinner. This is mine. Mine," she emphasized by pointing.

Peanut gave a lingering whine, followed by a short bark.

"I think we'll do both tonight. Peanut?" The perky ears twitched. "You and I will go for a walk. And, Princess?" Quick as a camera shutter, the wide eyes blinked. "When we get back, you and I will curl up on the couch. We can either read or watch a little TV."

Susan sighed contentedly and continued to eat, undaunted by the rapt attention she was receiving. They knew she'd leave a small portion for each of them in their dishes. These were the moments when they savored that expectation. And like them, she savored this time of the day too. After being around her clients or employees all day long, it was marvelous to have some solitude. Kim and Cindy probably imagined

Susan's life to be lonely, but it wasn't. It was meaningful. It was fulfilling. It was rich. It was everything she'd ever hoped for.

Chapter 7

On Sunday morning Evelyn sat in her customary pew—three rows from the rear on the right-hand side—and tried to concentrate on Pastor Masterson's sermon. He stood tall behind the elevated pulpit in his white pastoral vestment and stole. The Gospel lesson for the day was the doubting Thomas story from St. John, chapter 20.

"I remember when my brother John was only seven years old," the pastor was saying, "and I was ten. I was preparing to go on a camping trip with the scouting group. John was too young to go, and he was envious. He wanted to go in the worst way but, since he knew that he couldn't, he was trying to persuade me to stay home too. Somehow in his mind, it was easier to accept his exclusion from the trip if I was similarly excluded." He smiled.

"We've all been in similar situations, haven't we, with the roles reversed? When my brother was ten and I was thirteen, he got a larger Christmas present than I did. Funds were short that year and my parents, knowing that I was older and better able to understand, had explained it to me beforehand. 'John has his heart set on a GI Joe with the accessories,' my father told me. 'But if we buy that for him, we won't be able to spend as much money for your gift, Eric.'"

"I remember thinking, 'Maybe John should learn for once that he won't always get everything he wants.' But of course I didn't *say* that to my dad." He grinned. Laughter rippled through the cavernous sanctuary. "But aren't we all," he continued, "guilty of harboring that human characteristic of envy?"

"I think Thomas exhibits it very well in this chapter. Was he really as *doubting* as we've come to characterize him down through the centuries? Or was he simply envious that Jesus had chosen a time to appear to the disciples when he wasn't present?" He paused, making eye contact with those parishioners who were seriously contemplating his theory. He smiled and continued. "We know that Thomas was a courageous and devoted disciple. Twice, his words are quoted in other portions of this Gospel. In chapter 11, Thomas is willing to accompany Jesus even while expecting that the sojourn will end in death. 'Then let us go also,' he tells the others, 'so that we may die with him.' And after Jesus has described the place that is prepared for us in heaven, Thomas says to him, 'Lord, we don't know where you are going, so how can we know the way?' Thomas certainly didn't doubt that such a place existed. If he doubted at all, it was in his ability to reach it."

Pastor Masterson had a wonderful way of tying the Gospel lesson to the twentieth century. He often related childhood incidents that Evelyn found endearing. She could just picture what a sweet little boy he must've been, how proud he must've made his mother. And somehow by speaking of his childhood, he always tied the lesson to the present day lives of the adults present, though their ages varied significantly. For what adult there hadn't once been a child themselves? Or perhaps was struggling to raise their own children?

Evelyn glanced across the aisle to where Cindy Gunderson was seated with Gary and their three daughters. All were beautiful girls with their long blonde locks and soft blue eyes so like their mother's. Gary himself, had aged quite well too. His light brown hair hadn't receded too much for his forty years. Evelyn had heard that his farm was doing well. It was always kept so neat, the buildings in good repair with a fresh coat of paint applied before they appeared weathered.

A stab of remorse pierced Evelyn. She had been so sure that he and Susan would marry. They must have dated for almost a year and a half in high school. Of course she knew that they'd been young and that her hopes were likely ill-timed and ill-founded. And Susan hadn't seemed terribly disappointed when they'd broken up, so Evelyn was sure that she hadn't been so hurt as to swear off boys completely. But there'd never been another in the ensuing years that she'd ever really dated seriously.

Evelyn sighed. She'd come to accept years ago that Susan was happy with the way things were. Who was she to impose her own ideas upon another? Everyone was different. Just because she couldn't understand Susan's contentment didn't mean that it wasn't a fact. She'd learned that truth long ago with Nell.

Pastor Masterson's voice broke into her thoughts, and she tried to concentrate on his words.

"...any event, whatever the motivation for Thomas wanting to see the Lord himself with his own eyes, I think that his response once he did see him is most noteworthy. And what did Thomas say? 'My Lord and my God!' he said. There's that devotion coming through again. Yes, he doubted. But once his doubt was put to rest, he was right there at Jesus' feet, pledging his allegiance."

"And in that same text, we must also examine Jesus' response. 'You believe because you see. Blessed are those who believe without seeing.' Now, is Jesus ridiculing Thomas' need for proof here? Is he setting Thomas up as a disciple of poorer character because he required proof?" Pastor Masterson paused and made eye contact with several people in the congregation. "Not at all," he continued. "For if you look at the very beginning of the text, you'll see that the opportunity to question Jesus' resurrection was never presented to the others. Jesus had appeared, it says, and He willingly showed them His hands, His feet, His pierced side. In other words, with the other disciples, the proof that Jesus was indeed alive was standing right there before them.

So can one really lay any fault with Thomas for doubting when he was not even present?"

He had a point. Evelyn had never considered that before, but it was true. Jesus had never given the other disciples the opportunity to doubt. Thomas had been the only one, and he'd really behaved as any of the others might have if they'd been absent. Why then, had Thomas been singled out? Could it have been because of his devotion, because of his courage? And what were devotion and courage but faith, plain and simple? Had Jesus really used the situation as a chance to build Thomas' faith?

Taken in that light, doubt wasn't always necessarily a bad thing. This conclusion reassured Evelyn tremendously. Doubt was a natural reaction to the unexplained. Doubt was human. And God, having been human, understood it and used it to accomplish His will.

Kneeling at the communion rail near the end of the service, Evelyn still felt as though she'd received a revelation. The individuals on either side of her faded into obscurity. There was only her, Evelyn Justison, kneeling there and God before her—compassionate, understanding, and forgiving. The wafer placed in her palm, blurred through moist eyes. The wine glistened in the diffused light that seemed to bathe her. The blessing purged her soul. God understood, and God forgave her doubt.

As Evelyn mouthed the words to the closing hymn, her mind was elsewhere. It was true that she had harbored many doubts during her seventy-five years. But only one had forever haunted her until now—the one that questioned whether she had really been worthy of having a child. Had Susan been a shiny treasure, given to Evelyn only because her obsessive pursuit of such a prize had left God no choice in the matter? In the back of her mind, Evelyn realized that she had always harbored that conception. The proof had been in the fact that God had refused her next fondest wish—that of having a grandchild. It confirmed His ability to have the last say. At least that's what she'd always believed until today.

But today she realized, probably for the first time, God's enormity in every situation. He wasn't fallible like a parent, grudgingly giving in to a child's most adamant demands simply because His will wavered and He chose the easiest way out. He was omnipotent, in each and every situation. Nothing occurred that He hadn't foreseen eons before. Nothing occurred, even by human error, that God couldn't use to His own ends. Indeed Susan had been intended to be Evelyn's in the exact manner she came to be, from the beginning of time. For the first time since Susan's conception, Evelyn's doubt was erased.

"Mrs. Justison?" Cindy Gunderson's voice intruded from behind her as she was carried along by the slowly ebbing wave of worshipers.

Evelyn turned to see the face of her daughter's childhood friend smiling down at her radiantly. "Well hello, Cindy dear. How are you?"

"I'm just fine. Really busy with the wedding but loving every minute of it."

"Oh, I'm sure you are, dear. What a wonderful thing to see one of your daughters marry." Evelyn gasped. She hadn't intended that to come out as it sounded. Her mind had been elsewhere. Cindy was bound to take her remark to heart. "Forgive me, dear. I honestly did *not* mean that to sound as it did. I meant that weddings are a wonderful thing, and you're lucky to be so involved in the planning of your daughter's."

"I know." She took a deep breath as though gathering courage. "Mrs. Justison, I saw Susan at the grocery store yesterday. She seemed...well, I realized that she really is happy."

"Yes, she is."

"It sounds weird, but I never really noticed that before." She lowered her voice to a whisper and leaned closer to Evelyn's ear. "I think it's because I've always kind of felt...well, guilty."

Evelyn gazed into Cindy's moist eyes with understanding. "I know you have, Cindy, but there's no need."

She blinked and swiped quickly at her eyes, gaining control and beaming again her radiant smile. "Yes, I finally understand that. But I can't help wondering why Susan never comes to church. I mean...I always believed it was because she wanted to avoid Gary and I, but now that doesn't make sense."

"No, it doesn't, does it?" Evelyn had always wanted to know the answer to that question herself. Certainly Susan's faith had never seemed to falter, but long ago she'd quit attending church except for Christmas, Easter, and funerals. It hadn't been her place to ask why. Susan was an adult, after all. Cindy's question made Evelyn wonder again. But more than that, in light of her newfound revelation, Evelyn also wondered why she'd never felt it her place to ask Susan why. Good heavens. If a mother couldn't ask such an important question of her own daughter, who could? "I think perhaps she's just gotten lazy...would rather sleep in on Sunday morning."

Cindy nodded and squeezed Evelyn's hand. "Tell her that I miss her when you talk to her, okay?"

Evelyn continued to smile long after the young woman had turned her attention back to her family. Today seemed to be God's special day for revelations, and He wasn't just bestowing them on one Evelyn Justison.

A few minutes later, Evelyn parked her car in the resident lot behind Nell's 16-unit apartment building. She gripped the steering wheel of the silent car and stared up at the dark windows of Nell's apartment on the second floor. She'd known she would come here directly after church. She'd made the decision, with dread, the moment she'd awoken. What surprised her was that she no longer felt the dread. Instead she felt peace, as though God were sitting beside her offering encouragement. She sighed wistfully. What a remarkable, remarkable day this was turning out to be.

Safely inside, she snapped on the kitchen light beside the front door. The drapery-shuttered confines were bathed in an unfamiliar glow. Nell had never pulled the draperies. On a day as beautiful as this one, the windows would have even been cracked open. Evelyn would open everything up when she returned the next day to work. But she'd never been one to work on Sunday. Sundays were for rest, reading, and rejuvenation. And today, Sunday was for the eradication of secrets.

It wasn't surprising to find the objective of her visit in Nell's nightstand drawer. The surprise lay in the fact that it contained two diaries. Evelyn had always known that she'd kept a diary every year of her life since she'd been sixteen. Where in the world had she put them all? she'd often wondered. Then Nell had told her, shortly after her retirement, that she'd destroyed the lot of them except for the recap of their time in California. It made sense though, now that Evelyn considered it. Their sojourn to that state *had* encompassed two years, after all.

She stared at the leather-bound books in her time-weathered hands. Nell's words came back to her. "I want you to read that part of our lives, Evelyn, from my point of view. I think you need to if we're ever to understand each other."

"I will not relive it," Evelyn had argued adamantly. "It was too painful."

Nell had beseeched her further, but Evelyn had turned a deaf ear, shutting out her sister-in-law's pleas.

She reiterated her promise now as she stood alone in the bedroom that already smelled of disuse. Some events could only be faced once in a lifetime.

A short while later, Evelyn had returned home. She had just shut her own back door on the world when the phone started ringing. "Hello?" she answered.

"Hi, Mom. How was church?"

Evelyn took a deep breath, counting to ten. Susan asked that question almost every Sunday. But this was the first one in which Evelyn wanted to respond with "Why don't you come some Sunday and see for yourself?" Heavens, this wasn't like her at all. Nell's diaries had dredged up old bitterness.

"Mom? Are you there?"

"Yes, dear. I'm here." She prayed for calm and soft words. "Cindy Gunderson told me that she saw you yesterday."

"Yeah. We had a little chat in the grocery store. It reminded me of our old times together. I kind of miss her."

Evelyn's eyes widened. "Funny you should mention that. Those were the words Cindy told me to relay to you. 'Tell her that I miss her when you talk to her,' she said."

"Really?" Evelyn waited out the silence while Susan pondered. "Wow. I guess she felt it too."

"Felt what?"

"I don't know...what we've been missing all these years, I guess."

"Ah...I see. I got the impression that Cindy feels she's the reason you don't come to church very often."

"Cindy?" Susan's voice sounded surprised at the suggestion. "I don't think so. Maybe at first that might've been the reason. But sheesh! That's ancient history now."

"Yes, well. I suppose she had no reason to assume otherwise." Evelyn remembered her newfound resolution. "Why don't you come to church, Susan?"

"Wow, Mom. So direct. That's not like you."

"Why, Susan?" she persisted. There was a lengthy pause.

"Laziness, I guess. You get out of the habit, and it's hard to break back in."

Evelyn felt proud of herself after she'd replaced the receiver a few moments later. It sounded like Susan would indeed try to reinstill her old habit. And to think, it had taken no guilt or cajoling on her part. Just a concerned question.

But Evelyn also recognized that the peace she had felt in church had already deserted her. When had that happened? she wondered. And she realized that it had fled her when she'd opened Nell's nightstand drawer.

Chapter 8

Eric peered through the kitchen window again. The driveway was still empty. He must have heard John's rented car pull in a dozen times since he awoke this dismal and rainy Saturday. But each time he looked out, his brother wasn't there.

Why was he so anxious? he wondered. John had estimated his arrival time to be around 11:00 a.m. It was only a few minutes past that. John was a grown man, after all. He'd just turned forty in February. Old habits die hard, Eric decided. He'd spend his formative years looking out for his younger brother, and he'd probably do so until one of them died.

Tire-impacted wet gravel crunched outside the window. Thank God, Eric breathed as he lurched toward the sound and his eyes confirmed that he wasn't imagining this time. He shook his head with a smile. A red Mustang. Well, what else had he expected John to rent? The driver's door swung outward. John unfolded himself from the low seat and rose to his full height of six-two. Heedless of the dripping rain, he treated himself to a leisurely, reaching stretch. The dripping rain made rivulets in his lengthy blonde hair, and Eric noted that he now sported a neatly trimmed full beard, more light brown than blonde.

Eric met him at the kitchen door and held it open in invitation.

"Shitty weather," his brother greeted him.

Eric grinned. "It's been great until today."

"Figures." He entered and stomped the excess water onto the rug.

"I see you can finally grow a decent beard."

John eyed him suspiciously. "Thanks...I think."

Eric stepped toward him and wrapped him in a bear hug. John awkwardly returned it and pulled away first. He'd never been comfortable with outward displays of affection. "I'll bet you're hungry."

He shrugged. "Not really. I slid through a drive-through in one of the hundreds of towns between the airport and here. Man, you never told me there were so many. I never even got a chance to open her up. Every five miles there's another one, and they're all posted at thirty miles an hour. Sheesh! They all have little traffic cops orbiting around too."

"Maybe when the weather clears, I can show you a place outside of town where you can run it through the gears."

John's expression seemed skeptical. "Are you serious?"

Eric nodded. Man, did John think he'd turned into a nerd or something? He still liked cars. "Of course you'd have to give me a chance to drive it too."

His face lit in a devilish grin. "You're on."

Rapidly descending footsteps echoed from the staircase near the front of the house. A swooping shadow that was Kimberly launched through the dining room doorway behind them. "Uncle John!" she exclaimed and wrapped her arms around his neck.

His own enfolded her. "Kimberly, honey. Wow. You've grown up."

"Of course I have. We haven't seen each other in ages."

Eric realized with surprise that they hadn't seen John since the funeral.

"I can cook now and everything," Kim explained proudly as they released each other. "What's your favorite meal? I'll make it tonight for dinner."

"Ho boy. I don't know. Lemme think." He scratched his beard. "Do you do Mexican?"

Kim nodded a bit uncertainly. "I think so." Then with more determination, she declared, "Sure. Mexican it is." She turned to Eric.

"Dad? Can I have a ride over to Susan's? She invited me to bike over to see her today, but it's raining."

Eric was trying to figure out how Kim, usually so shy, had latched onto Susan so quickly when his brother spoke up. "Hey, Kim. I'll give you a lift. Does she live outside of town by chance?"

"No. On the other end."

"Well, that's okay. I'll give you a lift anyway."

During the short while that they were gone, Eric tried to determine the best way to approach the subject that was most on his mind. What had happened between John and Marcy? When John returned, he brought his two suitcases inside. Eric showed him to the bedroom that he'd be using, then left him alone to settle in. John came downstairs a short time later while Eric was sitting at the kitchen table eating a sandwich.

Straddling the opposing chair, John broke the silence. "I don't know what's up with Marcy. She's been all moody lately, crying more than she's smiling. I don't get it. I work hard. I'm not too unreasonable on what she wants to buy. I mean, she works too, so it's not like I've got all the say on how she spends it."

Eric held his tongue, practicing what he'd been preached in seminary—to be a good listener. He hoped his expression showed love and concern.

"I mean, I know what marriage is all about, what's expected of a good husband. It's compromise and commitment. It's life and reality...tough sometimes, but you work through it and try to make things better." He wearily ran his hands through his hair and settled his arms across the chair back. "I've done everything right, Eric. I've tried the best I can, but it's not good enough." He sighed heavily. "Two weeks ago, I came home to find her sitting in the dark just crying. I asked her what's wrong, and she says *everything*. She says it's not working, and she doesn't know what else to do, and she wants me to move out. She says we both need some time apart to decide if we still love each other."

He dropped his forehead to his crossed arms. "Jesus. She doesn't love me anymore."

Eric touched John's shoulder, but his brother continued to stare at his lap. "Did she say that?" he asked softly.

The downcast head nodded, then circled in a pattern signifying confusion. "I think so." His voice quivered with despair. "I was so shocked and angry that I can't really remember her words." He inhaled haltingly. "All my essentials were packed, she said. My friend, Craig, could take me in for a while, or I could find a place of my own if I wanted to. It was all planned. It was so...so...impersonal and strange."

Eric tried to picture the scene. It seemed unbelievable, not what he'd have expected from Marcy at all. "D...Do you think there might be someone else?" He held his breath, regret swimming over him at the question he'd just posed.

John's head surged up, and his green eyes were stormy as they pierced him. "No." The word was clipped and certain. "Marcy doesn't bullshit. If there was someone else, she would've shot straight and told me."

"I'm sorry, John. I believe you. I guess I'm just as confused as you are, and...well, I shouldn't have asked."

The face before him softened. "It's okay. I asked myself the same question and that's what I came up with. It's the one thing I believe without a doubt."

"Good." They sat in companionable silence for a long time. Eric wished he knew some magic strategy to suggest. He wished he were a marriage counselor. He even found himself wishing that he had some similar experience from his own marriage to share with his brother. It would bond them, make them both feel less alone and helpless. "It seemed to be going all right though?"

"Yeah. You know Marcy. She's pretty out there, pretty open. She'd been acting a little more depressed lately, but I figured...well, she was just going through one of those *stages*, like hormones or something."

Eric nodded. He understood a bit about depression. Sharon had experienced occasional bouts of it. "Did Marcy see anyone about it? There are medications that can level that kind of thing out."

He shrugged. "I don't know. She might have. It seemed like things were getting better before everything blew apart." He sighed. "I miss her. I miss the kids. I miss home."

Eric clasped his shoulder. "Hang in there, buddy." He tried to sound reassuring and confident. "It doesn't sound over yet. Maybe she realizes how much she misses you too. Separation isn't always the end you know. You'll both have a chance to think about yourselves, about each other, about your goals, your dreams. I wouldn't doubt that you'll both come out of this stronger than ever."

"But will we be together?" John's eyes stared into his own soulfully, as though he were God and knew the answer.

Shifting his gaze uncomfortably, he whispered, "I don't know, but we can pray that you will be."

Kim came home a half-hour later, carrying a grocery bag and explaining that Susan had given her a ride because she needed to finish the windows in their garage.

"But who paid for the groceries?" Eric asked her, suddenly struck by the irrational thought that Susan might be employing Debra Culpepper's tactics.

"I did. Susan paid me for helping her, and I bought them to make my welcome dinner for Uncle John."

"Honey, let me reimburse you." He reached back to lift the wallet from his pocket.

Kim swung away from the bag she was unpacking and glared at him. "Don't you dare! You'll ruin the present I wanted to give him with my own money."

He turned surprised eyes to his brother, who was his good-natured self again. John reclined languidly in the chair, arms crossed on his chest, a grin on his lips. "Women," he mouthed silently with an upraised brow.

That was for sure, Eric thought. Kim had never *told* him anything before. This was a new assertive side that he'd never seen. He decided it was either the influence of hormones or of Susan Justison.

Dinner was an extra spicy affair. Kim produced beef burritos from the oven and Spanish rice and refried beans from the stove. All were dosed a bit too liberally with hot sauce for Eric's taste. But John, always having a hearty appetite for the spicier things in life, devoured the fare enthusiastically. He poured the compliments on a blushing Kim as generously as she'd poured on the spices and the sauce. Eric grinned to see the two of them getting along so well. Mealtime hadn't been so much fun in a long time.

Marcus knocked on the door as they were all lending a hand to clear the table. He entered, encouraging Susan behind him to do the same. "Had to come over to meet the poor soul who had Eric here for an older brother," he said with a wink as he shook John's hand.

Eric made the introductions. "John, this is my friend Marcus. Behind him is Susan. Marcus and Susan, my brother John."

Susan hesitantly stepped forward and shook John's hand. She gave Eric an embarrassed nod.

Marcus explained, "I figured Susan here had slaved long enough in your garage. Told her it was time to come in out of the rain and say hello."

"I'm so sorry, Susan," Eric apologized. "I hadn't even realized you were still outside. You must be starved. Would you like something to eat?"

Before she could respond, Kim was whisking the leftovers to the microwave to reheat.

"Oh no, Pastor. That's really not necessary. I ate a late lunch."

"Nonsense. We have plenty." He turned to his friend. "Marcus? How about you? Hungry?"

"I hate to admit that I grabbed a bite before I left home. But it smells so good, I think I'll keep Susan company."

Kim, the perfect little hostess, had fresh settings of dinnerware and flatware on the table in record time. She insisted on starting the dishes while everyone else sat down at the dining room table. Susan seemed to relax quickly, and the conversation became lively and entertaining.

"That must be your rented five point o," she said to John as she dished up a small portion of rice. "Good taste. How's she do from zero to sixty?"

Eric caught John's surprised glance and smiled. "I believe the lady posed a question," he prodded his brother.

"Ah...I don't know. You've got so many little towns popping up every five miles out here that I couldn't find out."

"Too bad. I know a country road out of town where you could light it up."

Eric waved a hand in dismissal. "Already suggested by me. John and I have a date as soon as the pavement dries...providing he gives me a turn behind the wheel."

Susan glanced up and grinned in admiration. "Pardon me, Pastor. Didn't realize you were a hellion."

He felt his face redden. "I'm not, but I do like fast cars."

She nodded and winked at Marcus, seated across the table. "Well Father, you and I might have to go along to flag and scope. Wouldn't want the weekly paper full of the law-breaking antics of the Masterson brothers."

"Amen," Marcus concurred.

"Hey, what's this *father* stuff?" John asked in confusion.

"Marcus is a priest," Susan explained.

John's mouth gaped. "No sh...I mean, really?" He cast a scowl at Eric. "Thanks a lot, Eric. Man, I could've said something really...I don't know, sacrilegious or something."

Marcus laughed. "Chances are it wouldn't have been anything I haven't heard before."

Kim came through the kitchen doorway holding a dishtowel. "Hey everybody! I've got a great idea. Let's all play a game tonight!"

Eric's glance met John's. No doubt he was also remembering the Saturday nights when they used to play cards with the folks. "Sounds great, Kim. How about gin rummy?"

Susan eyed them both teasingly. "What? Not poker? And here I thought you two were confirmed juvenile delinquents."

"He's confirmed," John quipped, pointing at Eric, "and juvenile. I'm just delinquent."

Marcus and Susan howled with laughter and high-fived John across the table. Within a half-hour the table was again cleared of dishes and restocked with cards and score pads. Susan insisted they each cut for the deal, then won it with an ace. From that moment on, she seemed in control of the entire game. Eric would've blamed it on luck if he'd been stupid. But when she first lifted the deck, shuffled it at the speed of light, and then capped it off with that blurring trick he'd always marveled at…where the cards leapt from one palm to the other faster than the eye could see…well, he could only blame it on skill. Skill and possibly a bit of cheating. But then that required skill too. So skill it was.

Things were winding down by 9:30 when Marcus yawned and declared he'd been made a fool of long enough. Kim hadn't done too badly, finishing in third place. John held second. And Eric? Well, Eric trailed them all, which made him a bit irritable.

"Better luck next time," John encouraged him with a slap on the back.

"Oh, there's no luck involved," Susan explained. "Just ski—"

"Skill." Eric finished the sentence with a touch of sarcasm.

"Hmm." She turned to John. "Is he always such a sore—?"

"Always." Marcus took the response right out of his mouth.

After the visitors had finally taken leave and Kim had retired to her room, Eric trudged up the stairs with John. "Boy, that Susan is really something, isn't she?" his brother praised. "You know, she reminds me a bit of Marcy."

"Marcy. Would you mean your *wife* Marcy?"

John stopped on the upper landing and turned to stare at him like he was an alien. "Yes…Marcy, my wife." He crossed his arms. "Geez, Eric. What is *with* you?"

"Nothing is with me. I'm just reminding you that you're married."

He regretted his words the instant he saw John's green eyes ignite. "Don't worry," he spat. "I've lived lonely with the irony of that fact for the past two weeks."

"I'm sorry. Man, I didn't mean to say that." He reached out to touch John's arm, but he flinched away.

"Let *me* remind *you* of something, Eric." He punctuated his demand with a poke to Eric's chest. "I think you've forgotten that *you're* not." He continued to stare like he'd made a point of some kind.

"Not. Not what?"

John rolled his eyes. "Married. You're not married."

"Yeah? So? What's your point?"

He sighed in frustration. "Just forget it."

And with those words of wisdom, he moved down the hall to his bedroom and quietly closed the door behind him. As Eric did the same, he decided that, all in all, it hadn't been such a bad day.

Chapter 9

"Oh Susan," her mother whispered the moment she sat beside her in the pew. "I was beginning to worry that you weren't coming today."

The organ strained with the prelude for the opening hymn. Susan decided she'd better not cut it so close next week. She squeezed her mother's hand. "I told you I'd come."

Her mother beamed. "Thank you, dear."

It was humbling to realize that such a simple thing as coming to church could have made her mom's day. Susan wished she'd considered that years before.

The congregation had just joined in singing the first verse when Kimberly Masterson moved confidently up the center aisle. Her uncle John trailed behind her a couple of steps. He looked different than the evening before, all dressed up in a stylish navy suit with a flashy red and navy tie. It was funny how clothes could alter a person's impression of another. He made a pretty classy package. Kim had confided to her the previous afternoon that he and his wife were having problems. Susan hoped they could work them out. It was so disheartening to see a marriage break up.

Pastor Masterson stepped out of the sacristy to welcome everyone, and Susan was struck by a surreal feeling. It was the same face that had laughed and even pouted across the table from her the previous evening. But somehow when he wore his pastoral robe and stole, he seemed otherworldly, almost divine. She closed her eyes for a moment and opened them again. No, she wasn't dreaming. She still had that feeling. His clear voice resonated as he made some announcements. With her eyes closed, she could picture him in his khakis and casual shirt. But when she opened them, there was some other man standing there. Weird. She guessed it would just take a while to put the two apparitions together in her mind.

"Wasn't that a wonderful sermon?" her mother asked after the benediction.

"Just great," Susan lied. Not because it wasn't, but because she had no idea. She'd hardly listened to a word. The stained glass windows had captivated her, as they had when she'd been a child. The paraments had required her study after that. And finally, the different members of the congregation. She'd always marveled that Mr. Oldenberg could sleep so soundly with his back, neck, and head all so perfectly vertical. It was nice that things like that didn't change.

"Hi Susan," Kim greeted her from behind as they stood in the reception line to greet the pastor.

She turned and beamed a smile. "Hi Kim. I like your dress." It was a draping mini-floral pattern that cinched snugly around her trim waist and gave her a more mature appearance.

Kim blushed. "Thanks. I like yours too." Susan's was a larger floral pattern on a beige background. The bodice was slightly scooped and more hugging. The skirt was full and pleated.

"Yeah," John spoke up from behind Kim. "You clean up pretty well." He grinned. "Say, is your offer to scope, flag, or whatever still open?"

"Sure. Name the time."

"Two this afternoon."

"Great. Sunny Sunday afternoons are perfect for drag racing."

Susan's mother spun around and pinned her with one of her expressions that requested she keep her voice down. Both Kim and John noticed it and cast her a candid look of sympathy. It was hard to miss the underlying gleam in John's eyes though.

She tried to ignore her mother. "Better be sure to let Marcus know."

"Yeah. I'll have Eric get a hold of him."

Cindy Gunderson swooped around them and wrapped Susan in a warm hug. "I am so glad to see you here," she said. "Gosh, I'm so glad you came." She pulled away, her smile steady and certifying her sincerity.

"Me too, Cindy. We'll have to get together sometime soon. We've got a lot of catching up to do."

Gary stood behind her, grinning proudly. "I think I'm going to hug you too."

And he did, before Susan could even consider the appropriateness of the gesture. But it felt warm and brotherly—not uncomfortable in the least. And she decided that it made perfect sense. They'd been buddies since grade school. There were really more memories in their lifetimes than those of the short period they'd dated. As Susan looked over his shoulder, she was doubly blessed to see Cindy smiling in approval. Wow, she thought. What a cleansing moment.

"So Gary," she said after he'd released her. "Did you ever get the rear axle gears switched in your Boss 302?" He'd owned that Mustang since it was brand new in 1970. That was the year they all graduated. He saved every dime he earned for that car, and his parents paid for half of it as a graduation present. They'd already broken up by the time his dream had become reality, but Susan remembered that he always talked about the improved performance he'd get by making the modification. He gave it up as a daily driver shortly after he married Cindy. But on Sunday afternoons it was quite common to see the two of them taking it out for a spin.

He reddened. "You probably won't believe this, Susan, but no. I never got around to it. Although I did manage to find the time to give it one little modification."

She suddenly remembered the drag race set for that afternoon, and her face gleamed with her idea. "Think it'd whip a '93 five point o?"

"Hands down."

"Then bring it out to Swenson's quarter-mile at two o'clock...you and Cindy...and show us what she's got."

His eyes lit. "Really? You've got a drag planned? Who with?" Before she could respond, Cindy had tapped him on the shoulder and whispered something in his ear. Reality settled over him like a veil. "Ah shit. I forgot." He upended his palms. "Sorry," he told Susan. "We've gotta take the girls to St. Cloud for some more stuff for the wedding." Cindy whispered in his ear again and his eyebrow lifted. "That's a great idea," he told his wife. Turning to Susan again he explained. "Cindy suggested that you take the Boss out there for me and beat the pants off that '93."

She gaped while he pulled his keys from his pocket. He spun the ring until the oldest set worked free. Then lifting Susan's hand, he deposited it in her palm and pressed her fingers to enfold it. "My God, Gary. I don't know what to say."

"No need. Your face says it all. Make me proud."

Later, when she settled inside the car for the very first time, she marveled at its condition. Twenty-three years old and not a single flaw. The black shaker scoop rose up from the hood. The wide matching stripe, flanked by two narrower ones, raced down the sleek center. The rear window slats, the rear deck spoiler, the console, the tach—every option was on it. She slid out to do a walk around. Chrome Mags. A bright Grabber blue paint job. The perpendicular stripe crossing the hood, diving down the fenders, and streaking horizontally along both sides. Everything was magnificent. She slipped the key into the trunk latch and turned it. "Well, well, well," she noted as she peered inside. "A nitrous tank." That was definitely an ace up the sleeve. And that also explained the toggle switch under the dash. Hit the switch and instant turbo boost. Very nice feature. Not that she'd have to resort to such a tactic of course. She was confident in the Boss's stock abilities.

Everyone else had arrived at the straight paved county road known as Swenson's quarter-mile by the time Susan rumbled up. The stretch was more like a full mile long, but the traditional *track* began at the east intersection and ended at the Swenson driveway on the west. There was even a faded yellow stripe on the tar that marked the finish line. Marcus' late model Oldsmobile and John's rented Mustang were parked end to end along the right side near the starting line. Marcus, John, Eric, and Kim stood gawking as she pulled ahead of the row and stopped. She killed the engine and got out.

"Verrry nice," John drawled appreciatively as he strolled around it. "Looks like you want a *real* drag race, huh?"

"That's Gary Gunderson's Boss, isn't it?" Marcus asked.

"Yep. I'm doing him a favor. He told me to beat the pants off the '93."

Kim giggled excitedly, but her father didn't look too happy. "Ah...I don't know if this is such a good idea. I mean, you'll have two cars going side by side. Someone could come along and meet you head-on. And besides, that sort of thing isn't really legal."

"Ah c'mon, Dad. It'll be fun. Can I ride with in one of them?"

Eric looked tormented but before he could come to a decision, they all turned toward the sound of an approaching car. "Oh no," he said. "It's the sheriff."

"Relax," Susan assured him. "I went to school with Sheriff Hart."

He pulled ahead of the lineup and hoisted his husky frame from the driver's seat. "Where's Gary?" he asked.

Susan stepped forward. "He's not here. He let me take the Boss out this afternoon."

Andy Hart grinned. "Lucky you. Looks like you might be plannin' a drag here. Got a call from the Swenson's. They said somethin' was cookin' on this end."

Eric paled. Kim looked frightened. John stepped forward to explain, but Susan casually waved him back. "Yeah, we were, Andy. We only need to use it for about a half-hour. Can you just wait 'till we're done?"

If it were possible, his chest seemed to swell larger. He touched his hat brim, nodding once. "That's my job, Susie...to protect and serve, to wait if need be." He turned and slowly settled back into his patrol car. "I'll see you all at the other end." With that, he closed the door and drove off.

"Okay, I'm confused," John stated, scratching his beard. "He's going to go down to the end and what? Wait to arrest us?"

Susan laughed. "No. He's going to set up a roadblock with the sheriff's car so we don't get any unexpected company."

"Looks like we already have." Marcus had shielded his eyes and was peering to the west. The Swenson's old Impala was slowly making its way to the end of their driveway.

"Oh, they won't be a problem," she explained. "They'll just park at the end to watch the race."

"See Dad," Kim interjected. "Everything's legal, and we even have an audience. Now can I ride with Uncle John?"

Clearly, Eric didn't have much choice in the matter. Five minutes later, the '93 was idling in the right lane at the startup line, with John and Kim as its occupants. The Boss rumbled in the left lane, Susan behind the wheel and Marcus in the passenger seat. She'd wanted to go it alone, but he'd insisted that the passenger weight needed to be distributed equally between the opponents.

"Who's going to start us?" he asked after he'd buckled in. Eric had walked down to the finish line.

"Guess you'll have to get out," Susan suggested.

"Oh no. Not a chance." He rolled down his window and thrust out his arm. John glanced over and nodded. "You ready, Susan?"

She slipped the Hurst shifter into first. "Ready."

"On your mark..."

Susan flexed her fingers over the shift handle and eased out the clutch until it was a hairsbreadth from engaging.

"Get set..."

She glanced over and caught John's gleam of challenge in the other car. *Smile while you can*, she thought.

"Go!"

Clutch, throttle, roar, and thrust. The steady acceleration was such a rush! The tach rose—three, three and a half, four, four and a half.

"They're keeping up."

Five, five and a half, six. She should shift. Six and a quarter, six and a half.

"Susan."

Clutch, stick, clutch, throttle.

"Man, they gained a little there."

"Marcus, would you shut up?" She refused to glance over. Her peripheral vision gleamed red. Her ears roared with the horsepower.

"You're gaining now. C'mon, c'mon, Bossy!"

Six, six and a half.

"Susan."

Six and three quarters. Clutch, stick, clutch, gas.

"You're pushing it."

"She's got a good engine." And one more gear to go. She could do it. No nitrous needed. Fair and square. Six, six and a half, six and three quarters. Last chance. Clutch, stick, clutch, gas, gas, gas.

"Susan, I hate to say this—"

"Then don't, damn it. My pedal's to the metal."

"What's that switch down there for?"

Cheating, she thought. That switch is for cheaters. She was *not* a cheater. So close, so close, so close, but she wasn't going to cross first. Otis Swenson was leaping as high as his eighty years would allow him, waving his red bandana for the matching car that took it by a car length. "Shit!"

"A hundred and ten. Susan, slow down!"

"Shut up, Marcus." But of course, she did. It wouldn't have done to hit Andy's patrol car. They stopped far beyond John's car. Silence reigned when she cut the engine.

"What's the switch for?"

"Nitrous."

"Nitrous? Man, why didn't you use it?"

"Principles," she spat, pounding the steering wheel with each word. "Dirty rotten, ever loving, get you nowhere principles!"

"Well, I'll be damned."

And he may have been right. Marcus took the Boss against Eric in the second and final heat. Susan, Kim, and John watched with the Swenson's from the sidelines.

"What the hell was that?" John asked in astonishment as the Boss shot ahead to gain by two car lengths at the finish.

"That," Susan explained, "was a priest with no principles."

"Can you make it do that?" Kim asked excitedly.

Susan raised her voice to be heard over the argument that was ensuing between Eric and Marcus. "Sure I can," she said, suddenly realizing that the time for principles was past. "You talk your dad into letting you ride with me, and you can feel the g's from the passenger seat."

It required all Kim's power of persuasion, but she succeeded in her quest. A short while later, the two of them were roaring down the highway together. Perfect, Susan thought as she slipped it into fourth gear. The rapt audience of six waited just ahead, the sheriff having joined the Swenson's and the others.

"Flip the switch, Kim. Now!"

She did, and the boost set them both back in their seats. What a rush!

"You could've done that against Uncle John," Kim stated when they'd come to a stop. "But you didn't because it wouldn't have been fair. Right?"

"Yeah, I guess."

"Wow, Susan. You're the greatest!"

Suddenly Susan was enfolded in an awkward embrace across the console. Her own arms came around the girl and squeezed. And she realized that the flood of warmth inside her was better than the rush from the nitrous.

Chapter 10

The following Friday afternoon, Evelyn found it ironic to be going to the nursing home to be uplifted. But that's exactly what she found herself expecting—thanks to Hattie. All week she'd labored diligently at Nell's apartment. Susan had delivered a generous assortment of boxes, and Evelyn had spent the long hours in solitude—sorting and packing away a lifetime of the most precious memories. They were only the most precious, fortunately, because Nell had never been a packrat. And her auction ten years before, when she'd first located there, had dwindled the possessions even further. There were only two large boxes that Evelyn would keep for herself and Susan. The rest was of a household nature and could be given away.

"You look a bit glum," Hattie stated when Evelyn first walked into her room.

She passed the slumbering Adeline and sat wearily in the guest chair beside her friend. "Yes, I guess I am...that and tired." She sighed. "It's finished. I've gone through Nell's things and hopefully won't have to go back."

Hattie's hand came to rest atop her own and squeezed. "Lots of memories between the two of you. I can imagine how hard it was."

She nodded. "Lots and lots of memories, far more good than bad. She lived down the street from me even when we were little girls. I swear I spent more time at her house than my own some summers. It's odd to think we never lived further apart than a few blocks our whole lives."

"You were like sisters."

"Closer than that, I think. Even sisters eventually move away from each other. No, we were more like Siamese twins of an opposite nature." She gazed at Hattie thoughtfully. "Did you ever have a friend so close to you, who you spent so much time with, that you'd sometimes dream of getting away from them for a while?"

"Heavens, yes!" Hattie exclaimed with a slap on her thigh. "August."

"I beg your pardon?"

"August...Carlson...my husband."

The gleam in her eye was unmistakable, and Evelyn felt the mirth rise up inside her. When her laughter broke free it was like a circulating fountain, the polluted memories flowing out and the purified ones filtering back in.

"I love to hear you laugh, Evie. We need to get you to do more of that. Bust me out of here, and let's go have us some fun."

A smile still lingered on her face. "What did you have in mind?"

"The Land of the Ojibway."

She sobered. "What? You don't mean—?"

"You bet your sweet heart I do. You and me are gonna hit the casino." She rubbed her hands together eagerly. "I can hear those jackpot bells ringing already." Quick as a flash, she was wheeling ahead and out the doorway.

"But...really. I mean...I can't just pick up and drive all the way up to Mille Lacs. Why, I don't even drive after dark."

"Then we'll throw some things together and get us a room for the night. C'mon, Evie. Daylight's burnin'."

Evelyn still couldn't believe that she'd agreed to such a spontaneous and wild idea as they headed north on Highway 169. It had been Susan's fault, encouraging her to go for it when Evelyn had phoned her to explain Hattie's idea. But she couldn't deny the excitement that she felt either. She tried to remember the last time that she'd done something crazy like this and realized that it was before Edward had retired. He'd called her from the office one Friday morning and told her to have their bags packed by noon. He had them booked on the 6:00 p.m. flight to Las Vegas.

"What're you smiling about?" Hattie's teasing voice intruded on her thoughts.

She glanced in her rearview mirror to keep tabs on the traffic. It was a bit slow going. Everyone seemed to head north in Minnesota on a Friday afternoon. "I was just remembering when Edward and I took off just like this and went to Las Vegas for the weekend."

"You had a good time, huh?"

"It was marvelous...the lights, the excitement day and night, a whole different world."

"And not to mention the gambling."

"Oh, I don't gamble. That would be too wasteful."

"You don't gamble? Then why'd you go to Vegas?"

"Edward. He loved to play black jack."

"And you just sat there and watched him?"

"Pretty much."

"That sounds awfully boring to me."

"Oh, not at all. It was exciting. I'd watch the dealers beforehand and could often figure out which ones were unbeatable and which ones were having a stroke of bad luck."

"So you're saying that you'd tell your husband which tables to sit at?"

"I didn't have to. Edward could size them up pretty well himself. That man was a genius when it came to cards. He taught Susan and I to play several games. On Saturday nights at home, we often used to—"

"Hold on there, Evelyn. If you enjoy cards so much, why don't you give it a whirl today? Try your luck. If you're worried about blowing a wad of cash, just set a limit for yourself. You seem like a woman who can abide by her limits."

"Apparently not as well as I'd thought." She smiled at her friend who appeared confused. "If I could, I certainly wouldn't have agreed to a crazy trip like this. You seem to have more pull over me that way than even Nell had."

Throughout the remainder of the drive, Evelyn wondered why that might be? No one had been more persuasive for participation in her hair-brained schemes than Nell. Yet Evelyn had always stubbornly refused, even when she was sorely tempted. And she recalled now that she often felt a stab of jealousy when Nell related the good time she had on a weekend fishing trip, a road trip to some scenic place, or even an occasional classical concert in the cities. Why had Evelyn always refused her sister-in-law? Was it fear of situations with which she wasn't familiar? Or was it Nell herself and how Evelyn always felt that she faded into the woodwork in her presence? She'd have to table that to consider later. The exit to the casino was just ahead.

"Now Evie, you just pull up there by the front door and that nice-looking young man will have me out of here in a jiffy." She whisked a card from her purse and suspended it from the rearview mirror. "Here's my handicapped parking permit," she explained. "With this, you should be able to park your car real handy like."

Evelyn slowed to a stop beneath the lavishly lighted entry canopy. A handsome boy of about twenty-five politely assisted her in retrieving the wheelchair from her trunk. Within moments he had Hattie comfortably seated there. Evelyn had rolled her eyes at how helpless her friend had suddenly become in his presence, convincing the boy that he'd need to lift her into it.

"Cheap thrill," Hattie explained with a gleam in her eyes after he'd left.

"You're incorrigible," she scolded with a matching gleam.

The sights and sounds inside were every bit as exciting as Las Vegas. Rows upon rows of slot machines to their right as far as the eye could see. The discordant cacophony of coins falling, the pinging and whirring of the machinery, the laughter and conversation, the jarring bells that signaled a winner—they all conspired to make Evelyn feel disconnected for a moment.

"I like to play nickel draw poker," Hattie announced and wheeled away with purpose.

"Shouldn't we make reservations for the night?" Evelyn called after her.

Hattie spun around to face her. "Good idea. Would you mind taking care of that, Evie, since you're not gonna play? Then you could meet me back at the poker machines."

Evelyn agreed after obtaining more detailed directions as to where they'd meet. One last room was available that she reserved, although she was a bit astounded at the price. Apparently the exceptional rates that were advertised were only available on weeknights.

That done, she located her friend without too much trouble and stood beside her to observe. The draw poker machine, although quite clever, didn't hold her attention for too long. Nor did the other variety of machines that she saw. They were all so impersonal and repetitive. Before long she decided to walk down to the other end of the casino to see if it held anything of more interest.

The black jack tables were there, and she was drawn to them almost irresistibly. Here was something far more intriguing and challenging. All of the two-dollar minimum bet tables were full, as expected. What surprised Evelyn was that all the seats were occupied at the five-dollar tables as well. But the ten-dollar tables held a number of vacancies. A dealer at one of them seemed to be having a bit of bad luck. She stepped closer to study the situation.

Why was she always a spectator? she wondered. It occurred to her that it wasn't just games of black jack that she only observed. It seemed that, of late, she'd even become a bystander of life. Oh, certainly she'd never been a go-getter like Nell or like Hattie, but she used to be far more involved in it. It seemed now that she'd lost even that drive when she lost Edward.

With sudden determination, Evelyn moved to the cashier's window and purchased five ten-dollar chips. Before she could change her mind, she headed directly back to the table she'd been observing and took a chair. Only two other players were seated there—one on each side of her. They seemed relaxed and confident, so she tried to act the same way. She slid one of her chips into place to signify her bid and waited with baited breath for her cards.

Peeking at her hole card revealed it to be the nine of clubs. The next one that she was dealt, face up, was the ace of diamonds. The player to her right requested another card and broke with twenty-two points. Evelyn made a slight slashing motion before her to signify that she didn't want another card. The man on her left took another hit and busted with twenty-three. The dealer stayed and revealed his hole card—an eight to go with his king. Eighteen. Evelyn released her breath and revealed her twenty-point hand. She felt giddy as the dealer slid another ten-dollar chip across to her, but she tried to maintain a nonchalant expression.

Play continued with Evelyn surprising herself time and again. She lost a few but she won far more. One time she even doubled down when she split the two faces that she'd been dealt. Both queens gained her a simultaneous win at twice the profit.

"Now I see what you've been up to," Hattie spoke from behind her. "Winning a jackpot so you can treat me to a nice dinner."

Evelyn glanced down at the chips that had accumulated before her. Why, there was two hundred dollars' worth. Two hundred dollars! She'd increased her investment by three hundred percent in—How long had she been sitting here? "What time is it?"

"Dinner time, and you're buyin'. Pack up those chips and let's go cash 'em in."

She had a surreal feeling throughout their steak meal at the casino's adjoining restaurant. How had the afternoon passed so quickly? How had she been so fortunate as to win? Suddenly it was obvious how people could become so hooked on the pastime of gambling. Was she in danger of that? No, she determined. She would have quit if her chips had run out. And since she'd already decided that the firsthand experience of black jack was worth the fifty dollars that she invested, her experiment would have been a success even if she'd failed.

Just as Evelyn had resolved herself to accept her momentary lapse in prudence, another bombshell was dropped upon her. The hotel had overbooked and accepted her reservation in error. There were no double rooms in the inn. Evelyn felt shell-shocked with the very idea of driving over a hundred miles to reach the safety of her own home in Crow River. Her night vision had all but deserted her years ago. When she glanced down at Hattie, beside her before the reservation desk, she knew her fear was evident in her expression

"It's okay, Evie," Hattie whispered. "Just leave it to me."

Then before her very eyes, her proud and confident friend seemed to shrivel into a helpless invalid. She slumped within her chair as though the starch had fled her spine. Her hands folded back upon her wrists, fingers jutting and jerking as though she was suffering a seizure of some sort. In a loud but slurring voice she declared, "I'll drive us home, honey. I know you're as good as blind behind the wheel in the dark."

The desk clerk leaned over the counter to see who had spoken. Her mouth gaped. Her shocked gaze met Evelyn's, who shrugged dismissively. Within fifteen minutes they were being escorted into a luxurious three-room suite, the likes of which Evelyn had never imagined in her wildest dreams. Sunken living room, French doors opening into the bedroom, a spacious bathroom, complete with a Jacuzzi—and all for the price of a normal room.

Hattie maintained her pathetic ruse until the instant the door closed on the exiting staff member. Then she collapsed again, but this time into an uncontrollable fit of laughter. Evelyn couldn't help but join in and found herself seated on the floor at her friend's feet when it was all over.

"What're you waiting for?" Hattie asked with glee. "Let's hit the Jacuzzi."

"But I didn't bring a swimsuit."

"Who needs a suit?"

"Certainly you're not suggesting that we bathe in the…in the—"

"Nude? Oh, all right, you party-pooper. Did you bring an extra bra and underwear?" Evelyn nodded. "Good. Then you can just wear the ones you've got on. So what if they get wet?"

What a splendid idea, Evelyn thought. But as she took the first turn in the bedroom to undress, she was struck by another more sobering one. "Hattie?" she called through the doorway. "Did you bring extra underthings too?"

Her friend barked with laughter. "Yep. That I did. You're safe with me, Evie."

Later, when they were lying side by side in the elegant king-size bed, Evelyn realized that she hadn't felt so free and happy in years. A whole world existed with tiny pleasures that she'd never dared to try. Today she'd taken the first small step.

Was it because of Hattie? she wondered. Without her influence, would Evelyn be forever doomed to her predictable and mundane existence? That was certainly a possibility. If she had dared to share in a bit of adventure with Nell years ago, would she have learned by now to do so of her own accord? If that were true, it was a shame to think of the years wasted by her stubbornness.

"Evie? Are you awake?"

"Mmm hmm. Just thinking about all the fun I've had today."

"Me too, and I wanted to thank you for it."

"Thank *me*?"

"Yeah. There's not many women I know who'd put up with my shenanigans like you did today."

"I think they're very refreshing."

"Really?" Hattie's hand moved over her own and squeezed. "Thanks Evelyn...for everything."

Tears filled her eyes as she squeezed Hattie's hand in return. Would Nell have felt just as grateful if they'd spent a crazy day together like this? She suddenly knew the answer without a doubt. Yes, she would have. Evelyn was chagrined to think that she'd never even considered that possibility before. Outgoing people like Nell didn't need a conservative friend like her. That's what she'd always assumed. But now, because of Hattie, she realized that they did. How could she have been so blind to that truth? Had she really known Nell as well as she'd always thought? Apparently not. The loss gripped her with a lonely pain in her heart. The time was past now. Nell was gone.

In the hazy state between wakefulness and sleep, Evelyn distantly recalled the diaries and realized that they held the key to knowing Nell even now. And just before unconsciousness claimed her, she vowed that she would read them. She'd face the demons of the past that lurked within them if only for another chance to know the real Nell.

Chapter 11

The telephone on Eric's study desk shrilled at nine o'clock on Saturday morning, the first of May. He absently reached for it as he penned another thought on his sermon notes. "Pastor Masterson."

"Eric? This is Marcy."

He would've recognized his sister-in-law's voice without her identification. Relief swept through him. Perhaps she was ready to reconcile. "How are you?"

"Okay, I guess. No, that's not true. I've been better."

"I'm sure. Listen, I really hope that you and John can work things out. I'd hate to lose you."

"Me too, but…well, it's going to take some time apart. I'm still sorting things out."

"I understand." He knew he was lying, but he said the words anyway. He didn't understand at all. What did she need to sort out, and why did she have to do it alone? Shouldn't a couple sort things out by talking? He and Sharon always had. But whenever John had called Marcy, she'd cut him short and put the kids on. "Is there anything I can do to help?"

"Thanks. But no. I've gotta do this myself."

"He misses you."

There was a lengthy pause. "I miss him too. But does he miss *me*, Eric, or just the comfortable routine we had?"

"I'm sure both."

"Yeah, well, I don't know. That's the problem. I just don't know anymore if *I'm* the most important thing in his life, or if he's just plugging along because he's comfortable with the status quo."

"Maybe if you'd talk, the two of you could—"

"We will, but not yet. I...I just need some more time."

"Okay."

"Is he there? I wanted to ask him something."

"I'm afraid not. He and Kim went for a drive. Can I have him call you back?" He waited a few heartbeats before she spoke.

"Would you just ask him this for me? I'm heading out the door, and he can just call back and leave a message on the machine."

"Certainly."

"Just ask him if he still intended to make the house payment like usual, or if I should budget it into my expenses."

Eric felt anger well up that he quickly quelled. She sure had a lot of nerve, kicking his brother out and still expecting him to pay for a roof over her head. "I'll relay the message." He knew his voice sounded cool.

"Thanks. I'll probably talk to you soon."

"Goodbye, Marcy."

He heard the rear screen door open just as he'd replaced the receiver. Footsteps raced through the house to his study.

"Dad! John let me drive!"

Eric shot up and glared at his brother, who stood behind Kim. "Are you crazy? She's only thirteen!"

He shrugged. "Relax. It was a gravel road, and I just taught her how to shift gears a little."

"It's illegal."

"C'mon. There's farm kids living around here, probably younger than her, who are driving."

"I don't care! She's not a farmer's daughter. She's the minister's."

John crossed his arms and leaned against the door jam. "Is *that* what this is all about? Your reputation?"

Eric strode around the desk, eyes locked with John's, until they were face to face. "How dare you."

"Daddy, I'm sorry. It wasn't Uncle John's fault. I wouldn't take *no* for an answer. I kept begging, and he finally let me."

He glanced down at his daughter's worried expression and forced himself to calm. "It's okay, honey. No one's to blame. Neither of you knew how I'd feel about it." He smiled. "Why don't you occupy yourself elsewhere for a while so I can talk to your uncle."

Her eyes narrowed. "You're sure you're not mad at him?"

"Kim, you know me better than that. I never get mad."

She reluctantly exited the room. Eric closed the door behind her and faced John. "I'm sorry that I overreacted. It just reminded me of Kyle and the accident. In my eyes, even fifteen is too young to drive."

"Man, I'm sorry, Eric. I never even thought of that. I promise it won't happen again."

Eric nodded. "Marcy just called."

His brother's face lit. "Did she want me to call back?"

"Ah...sort of. She was going somewhere, but she said you could leave your answer on the machine."

His smile faded. "To what?"

"Ah...she was wondering if you still intended to make the house payment." Eric waited for the outburst, but John didn't look the least bit upset. "What are you planning to tell her?"

"Sure. That's the deal. I pay for the house. She pays for the utilities."

"But you don't live there."

"Geez, Eric. It's not permanent. I'll be moving back some day...hopefully soon."

He shook his head. "It just doesn't seem right."

John gave a short laugh. "Of course it doesn't...to you. You and Sharon didn't have the kind of marriage that Marcy and I do."

"What's that supposed to mean?"

"Forget it." He turned to leave.

"No wait. I don't want to drop this. What did you mean?"

John paused and tipped his head back, staring at the ceiling. Finally he turned to face Eric again. "You and Sharon had an old-fashioned, traditional marriage. You were the breadwinner, and Sharon was the homemaker. That's cool. I'm not saying it's not, but that doesn't work for many women these days. I know it sure wouldn't work for Marcy. She's too driven. I wouldn't be able to satisfy all her needs if her whole world revolved around me and the kids. And that's okay too. I don't think I'd be satisfied with a woman who was satisfied with that."

"What are you saying? That Sharon was less of a woman?" Eric felt his temper rising again.

John sensed it and raised his hands in surrender. "No, Eric. I'm not saying that at all. Sharon was a wonderful woman. She was a perfect woman, really. I never knew a woman with such an even temperament...so patient and kind to everyone. You must've done a wonderful job of keeping her happy. I...I'm really sorry she's gone."

Eric felt the stabbing pain again of her loss and forced it away. He clasped his brother's shoulder. "Me too."

"All I was trying to say was that...well, Marcy and I are used to living differently. We're committed to the way that works for us. I mean, say if I was to quit making the house payments, and we got back together later. I think I'd always wonder if she took me back just because it helped with the finances, you know?"

"I can't believe that would be the only reason."

"Yeah, well, on my good days that's how I can look at it too. But on the bad days... I'm just not that secure."

Eric wrapped his free arm around him and pulled him in for a hug. John patted his back awkwardly and moved away a moment later.

"My vacation time's almost up, and I've decided I can't go back to Chicago unless it's to my own place. I won't impose on Craig there, and I won't impose on you either. I...ah...called my boss, and he said that my job'll be waiting no matter when I come back. 'Course he can't pay me beyond my vacation, so I took an extended leave of absence.

Anyway, I need a job for a while...here." He grinned sheepishly. "Do you know anyone who needs a carpenter?"

Eric still felt a little indignant that his sister-in-law would reduce his brother to begging for employment. "I'm sure Susan could give us some leads."

"Great. And she might know about some places for short-term rental too."

"Why would you need that? You're welcome here for as long as you need it."

"I know." He smiled sincerely. "And thanks. But I need my own space, you know? A person kind of gets used to their own ways and well, one week is enough to wear out a person's welcome anywhere."

Eric sat alone in his study for a long time after John had left to use the phone upstairs. His sermon notes lay before him unheeded, his mind occupied by other thoughts. Something his brother had said struck a sour cord with him, and it took him a while to discern what it was. He was jarred from his reverie by a slight commotion in the kitchen. Glancing at his watch, he was surprised that it was already ten o'clock. Marcus was right on time as usual.

"Ready to go?" his friend asked from the open doorway. The two of them planned to take in a car show in River Valley.

"Not quite. I'd like your opinion on something first."

"Go ahead. Shoot."

Eric motioned him to the guest chair while he remained behind his desk. He briefly explained the morning's events—Marcy's call, John's response, their ensuing conversation, and John's plan to get a temporary job and move out. "Something he said bothers me though. John said, 'You must've done a wonderful job of keeping Sharon happy.' What does that mean? What makes a woman happy? I never did anything special."

Marcus rested his ankle on his other knee. "I'm not really an expert on this, but I *have* had some experience with similar questions during our marriage encounter classes. We've asked the men what they think their wives need from them. The responses are pretty interesting. The more...oh, I'd call them *macho men*, usually respond with a list of material things or a list of rules like *showing up for dinner on time*. But I think the more sensitive men are closer to the real answer. They often mention more emotional concepts like *praise* and *appreciation*."

"I *think* I did that with Sharon."

"I'm sure you did. You're a considerate person."

"But I'm not sure now. She was being treated for depression when...when she died. I'm asking myself *why*? Was it something I might have contributed to?"

"Eric, why do you torture yourself like this?"

"I don't know." He propped his elbows on the desk and rubbed his temples. "John and Marcy were married the same year as Sharon and I. A year and a half ago, I never would've imagined that this could happen to them. If Sharon were still alive, would we be having problems now too?"

Marcus stared at him silently with sympathy in his eyes.

"I know. It sounds irrational to be thinking like this, doesn't it? I guess it just got me thinking, wondering if I was as good to Sharon as she deserved. It's a moot point now, so it's a waste of effort to agonize over it." He sighed. "Let's get going to that show."

"Sounds good." Marcus stood and stretched. "But Eric? Just for the record, regardless of how wasted the effort, if you need to talk again, I'm here for you."

Eric came around the desk and gave his friend a short embrace, ending with an affectionate pat on his back. "Thanks, Marcus. I appreciate it."

As they were exiting through the rear door, Susan Justison's pickup pulled in the driveway. She stopped and got out, smiling with her usual enthusiasm.

"Are you here for Kimberly?" Eric had accepted the fact that his daughter had latched onto Susan as her mentor.

"Sure, if she wants to ride along. John called, and I'm here to take him over to see Nell's apartment."

"Wow. He works fast. He only mentioned it an hour ago."

"Well, it's a good thing he called when he did. It's still got the furnishings and the household goods inside. I was thinking of hauling them out today. If he likes it, I'll keep them there for the time being."

"Did he ask you if you knew of anyone who might need a carpenter too?"

"Yep. Got that covered. I can put him on my crew for a while."

"Thank you, Susan. That's very generous of you."

"Hah!" she said with a laugh. "Nothing generous about it. If he works for me, he'll have to work his butt off."

"Amen to that," Marcus interjected. "Your brother just signed on to the slave ship."

John came up behind them. "What's this about a *slave ship*?"

"They're talking about your working for me. Marcus thought he was being clever." She grinned at Marcus. "Can't blame a girl for wanting to stay afloat and make progress." Turning back to John, she asked, "Does Kim want to come with us?"

"Nah. I asked her, but she's got some special meal planned that she wants to start on."

Eric stared after them as the pickup backed out of the driveway. Something bothered him about seeing the two of them together. Susan was too much like Marcy. Given John's current situation, he didn't like the combination of proximity and loneliness.

River Valley was a fifty-mile drive north on a lazy two-lane highway. The weather was mild but overcast with no hint of rain. That boded well for the outdoor show. Conversation was minimal along the way. Marcus seemed to sense Eric's need to think and only interrupted with an occasional polite comment about the scenery.

Eric was ruminating, being sucked deeper into thoughts of his life with Sharon, when he forced his mind to surface and take in his surroundings. A sharp curve lay dead ahead, and Marcus, in his usual manner of dare-devil driving, didn't slow down much. Eric tensed and all air escaped his lungs. The view blurred into a kaleidoscope of speeding colors as his body was forced toward the door with the momentum of the turn. The car came out of it flawlessly and straightened with the highway. But it took several moments before Eric felt as though the centrifugal pressure had eased and his vision had cleared to discern singular trees and fence posts. He expelled a long breath of relief.

"Are you all right, buddy?" Marcus glanced at him in confusion. "You look a little peaked."

He gave a short laugh. "You should drive in the Indy."

"C'mon." He grinned. "Give me a break. My wheels never left the ground."

Eric grinned but he still felt a little ill. Naturally Marcus wouldn't know the reason. He'd never told him that Kyle and Sharon had been killed on a curve just as sharp, with a stunt just as unnecessary. But unlike Marcus, whose execution included years of driving experience, Kyle had only held a learner's permit. And Sharon shouldn't have been the parent seated in the passenger seat. He should have been.

Chapter 12

By Friday afternoon Susan had decided that John Masterson was a godsend. His move into Nell's apartment had been timely. Not only had it postponed the disposal of the remaining contents, but it had also eliminated her need to repaint the interior. He'd been more than willing to do that himself in exchange for a month's free rent. She figured it was a fair arrangement. Two less things to worry about right now.

John's contribution to her work crew, however, had a greater impact than she'd every imagined. He was phenomenally skilled—both in rough and in finish carpentry. It was easy to understand why his boss in Chicago had agreed to an extended leave of absence. Employees of John's expertise and conscientiousness were rare commodities.

By the end of the first day on the job, John had easily won her respect. But more importantly, he'd been accepted by the others. Marvin—soon to retire—seemed to be relieved that he didn't have another greenhorn to break. And Kevin and Andy seemed pleased to take instruction from a mentor who possessed a little more patience than Marvin.

"What'chu got planned for tonight, Susie?" Marvin asked as they knocked off for the week at the duplex.

"A nice long bath and a good book."

"Sounds like a helluva boring way to spend your fortieth birthday."

She reddened. Darn Marvin. Why did he have such a good memory?

"Now you know I'd never forget your birthday, Susie. It's the day after Caleb's."

She remembered that his grandson had been born just before her thirty-fifth birthday. "So Caleb's five already? Wow. Time flies."

"That it does. Faster every year." He fixed her with his hazel eyes. "Even when you pretend that the birthdays are just another day."

"I wasn't pretending. I just don't have any special plans until tomorrow when Mom and I are going out to dinner."

Marvin tisked. "That won't do at all. The boys and I already decided that we'd take you out if you didn't have nothing planned." She started to protest, but he waved it aside. "You just go home and soak in that tub. We'll pick you up at 7:00 and head to Dandy's for a while."

Susan was pleased to see Marvin's wife, Dorothy, waiting in their Jeep Cherokee when he called at her front door. Dorothy was a buxom but petite woman with an ever-present sense of humor.

"How're you doin', sweetie?" the older lady greeted her as Susan climbed into the back seat. Before she could respond, Dorothy continued. "The big four-o calls for a big celebration. Shame on you. Marvin said you were plannin' on spending it alone."

She explained her plans with her mother for the next day.

Dorothy scolded her again with a twinkle in her eyes. "So you were gonna forget all about your poor friends? Marvin never takes me anywhere, you know. Secluded woman like me needs an excuse to get out and visit once in a while."

Susan laughed along with her. Dorothy was as far from secluded as they came. She had her two cents worth in more committees that anyone else in Crow River. If you needed something accomplished for the improvement of the town, you just called Dorothy and it would be done.

Dandy's was a spacious bar and grill on the south side. A recent addition to the back had provided a banquet room that seated a hundred easily. But the front retained the coziness that Susan had always remembered—being divided into three smaller alcoves. One contained a pool table, electronic dartboard, and two pinball machines. Another contained a U-shaped bar with the expanded kitchen facilities behind it. And the third, where the rest of the gang including Kevin and Andy's wives already waited, contained ten tables for four. Three had been pushed together to accommodate their group of eight.

It had been a similar, but smaller, group that had celebrated her thirtieth birthday with her. Marvin had instigated that affair as well. But since her crew at that time had included only one other man who had since retired, they'd only taken up two tables. Susan felt warmed in her heart, as she had then, to see everyone relaxed, joking, and toasting in her honor. Good friends really made life worth living.

"To Susan," Marvin saluted with an upraised Miller bottle. "The orneriest boss I've ever had." He winked and glasses clinked together.

"To Susan," Kevin spoke next. "The *only* boss I've ever had."

"Now that isn't exactly true," Andy corrected. "You used to detassel corn like everyone else around here."

"What's that mean...*detassel corn*?" John asked. "You actually take the tassels off the corn?"

"Not all the corn, only the female rows."

"You're telling me there's male and female corn?" John's face looked incredulous.

"Yep. In the seed corn business there is."

"Wow. I never knew that."

"'Course you didn't," Marvin teased. "You're just an ignorant city slicker."

John grinned. "Guilty. But I'm a fast learner."

"That you are," Marvin agreed. "Took no time at all to teach you how to trim off and support that drop counter in the kitchen."

The crew laughed in unison since it had been John who'd shown Marvin how to shape the supporting oak pieces in a practical but decorative manner.

Conversation continued good-naturedly through the meal and the rest of the evening. The women maintained their own discussion at their end of the table. Kevin's wife, Katie, had her three-month-old son to rave about and photos to show. Dorothy provided her with maternal advice. And Kristy, Andy's wife, declared that they planned to wait another year or two before starting their family.

"That's a good idea," Katie commented. "Your life really changes with a baby. It's best to be ready for the responsibility."

"Sometimes I wonder if I'll ever be ready. But then I get to wondering what a baby we'd have would look like. Would he look like Andy?" Kristy's eyes turned dreamy. "Gosh, it'd be neat to have a little Andy depending on me."

"But that's a pretty short-lived affair," Dorothy interjected. "Before you know it, they're teenagers and think their parents are the dumbest human beings on earth."

"When does that change for the better?" Katie asked with wide-eyed interest.

Dorothy hooted. "Beats me. I'm still waitin'. But I'm thinking little Caleb might make the difference with his daddy. Why, just last week our son was asking Marvin about life insurance policies, wondering what kind were the best to provide his family with economic security. Lord, I never would've guessed that I'd see that day."

Susan had never stopped to think before about the drastic change wrought in the lives of new parents. Suddenly even the most carefree of spirits was forced to face the fact that another human being was depending on them for their very sustenance. Certainly marriage itself couldn't be as traumatic. There you had two independent people, each capable of making it on their own if the need arose.

What held marriages together during those busy years of child raising? The mutual need to provide for the children? It must be far more than that, she decided. Certainly love played a big part. She'd seen the example of that in her own parents. But what was love really? Definitely not the sappy feeling she'd experienced as a teenager with Gary.

One seldom saw married couples holding hands or walking arm in arm. And that was the real shame of it all as far as Susan was concerned. She'd seen the outward signs of infatuation fade in couples of her own age group, and she wondered why? Why could two people, once so enamored of each other, become only two people who peacefully co-existed? Why did they seem to take each other for granted?

Far too soon the evening was over. Susan noticed Katie give Kevin a significant gaze across the table. Kevin immediately discerned its meaning and rose, making his apologies that they'd have to be going. It was almost 11:00 already, and their son was an early riser.

Katie wished Susan a warm happy birthday as they departed. It was so wonderful, she explained, to have a good reason to get a sitter. She and Kevin hadn't been out together like this since little Linden had been born.

Susan watched them as they moved through the doorway. Kevin's arm came up around Katie's shoulder, where he tucked her securely under his own. There it was, Susan thought with a sudden stab of envy. That little teenage show of affection, tempered with a maturity gained through trial.

"I suppose we'd better get going too," Andy was saying. "Happy birthday, boss."

She smiled, accepting their well-wishes as he and Kristy took their leave. Andy's arm slipped protectively around his wife's waist.

A chair clattered to the tile floor. Her gaze swung to take in the cause. John stood unsteadily, then reached down awkwardly and set it aright.

He reddened. "Sorry. Guess I had a bit more than I thought."

"No problem." Marvin smiled to ease his discomfort. "Dorothy and I will give you a lift home too."

"Can't leave the Mustang." The firm shake of his head left little room for argument.

"How about if I drive your Mustang?" Susan suggested. She'd been drinking only Coke after the initial toasts. "I'll drop you off and bring it home for the evening. Tomorrow morning I'll bring it back to your place and walk home."

"This is embarrassing," John said as he buckled his passenger seatbelt a few moments later.

"What? Having a woman drive you home?" She started the engine, checked traffic, and pulled out.

"No. Needing a ride home in the first place. Honest, I'm not much of a drinker. And if I do, I know my limit."

"I believe you."

"Good. I'm not saying it was always that way, but a guy's gotta grow up sometime."

"When did you grow up?" Only the accelerating motor greeted her question. She glanced his way to see that his face was pale.

"Whew," he muttered. "Mind if I open the window a little?"

"Be my guest."

He depressed the button until it slid all the way down, then hung his head outside for a block and a half. He drew it back in. "Much better. Now, what did you ask me before?"

"When did you grow up? I mean as far as drinking and driving?"

"Ah." He sighed, sounding much more in control of himself again. "That would be the time when my oldest was just a baby. I was arguing with Marcy, insisting that I'd bring the babysitter home when wham!"

"She cold-cocked you?"

"Nope. I just passed out. Woke up in the bathroom a little while later, sick as a dog. I was alone because Marcy had taken Jeb with her while she drove the sitter home. I remember thinking that could never happen again. I was a dad now. I had responsibilities. I had to quit acting like a proud and stupid kid."

Susan turned into the parking lot of his apartment building and pulled into the space closest to the door. She cut the engine. "I was just thinking about that tonight. About how much responsibility a family must put on a couple."

"Yeah. It does. But you're in it together and it's worth it."

"I'm sure it is, so long as you don't start taking each other for granted."

"How do you mean?"

"Oh, I don't know. I've watched friends my age who seem to grow so used to each other that there's no romance left. They seem more like a brother and sister together. Some have split up and some just keep plodding along like that."

"That's understandable really. Life is no picnic. You're deceiving yourself if you think a marriage can persist on all that mushy stuff."

She tipped her face against the headrest and stared at him. "Am I?" She sighed. "I just saw evidence to the contrary tonight. Kevin and Katie, and Andy and Kristy…they walked out of Dandy's arm in arm."

"So? Maybe Kevin and Andy were too drunk to walk out of there without leaning on someone."

Susan caught the gleam in his eyes just in the knick of time. She was ready to loose a barrage of verbal abuse on him for his callous, chauvinistic attitude. "Yeah," she replied dryly. "That must've been it. Why else would they put their arms around their wives?"

"No, seriously, Susan. They're young yet, but they'll outgrow that. As you get older, you shouldn't need to do all that stuff or even say all that stuff. Your actions, like your chores around the house or your contribution to the family income, should say enough."

She searched for the gleam in his eyes but there was none. John was dead serious. Suddenly she understood what his wife's actions in kicking him out might have been saying. The poor woman was probably starving for some loving affection from him. She bit her tongue. It certainly wasn't her place to speak her opinion. He was her employee, and she was definitely no expert on marriage. "Well, do you need someone to lean on to make it to your door?"

"No sir…I mean ma'am…I mean boss—"

"Agh! Get out of here then and quit kissing up!"

"Okay, but I've gotta ask you one very important thing. The car…when were you gonna bring it back?"

"Tomorrow morning. Soon enough? Now get outa here!"

A half-hour later, Susan had just settled into her comfortable bed with her cat snuggled contentedly against her armpit. She was fading out when the doorbell chimed, startling her awake. Coaxing wouldn't persuade the cat to move, so she lifted the obstinate feline and thrust her aside. Princess mewled in protest while Susan slipped into her short wrapper and shuffled to the door. She peeked through the peephole and opened it inward to a red-faced Eric Masterson.

"Where is he?" he asked.

Her confusion was evident. Why would Eric concern himself with her dog, Peanut? "I don't know. My guess is *under the bed*. He probably dived there when you rang the bell."

Eric brushed her out of the way in a rage. "Where is it?"

"Where is what?" She hurried to catch him as he strode down her hallway.

"The bedroom."

He found his destination, apparent by the unmade bed, and flipped on the light. Flopping down on his stomach, he lifted the bed skirt and peered beneath it. A shrill bark erupted. On its heels was a painful human yowl. Eric emerged with claw scratches across his nose. "Where's John?" he demanded of her, cupping his beak.

Now she was more confused than ever. "John? He's home in his apartment."

Eric stood, dropping his hands to his hips. "But his car is in your driveway."

Susan gaped at him, the ramifications of his accusation finally hitting home. And her hand, in complete accord with her wishes, snapped his judgmental face aside with a reeling slap.

Chapter 13

Evelyn glanced at the alarm clock on her nightstand. Eleven o'clock already. Goodness. She'd been reading for two hours and would be dragging for church in the morning. She forced herself to shut the diary. After locking the clasp, she slipped it under her Bible in the drawer. Snapping off the light on the headboard, the room was plunged into darkness, save the weak stream from the hallway nightlight. Evelyn fluffed her pillow and slid further beneath the covers.

It had been this way all week—the consuming desire to read further, the inner battle to set the diary aside. Nell had been a wonderful writer. Her narratives held such depth, such enticement, so much of herself. It was odd how surprising that had been to discover. Certainly Nell had been an English teacher, but Evelyn had never realized the creativity that her sister-in-law possessed to accompany the grammatical rules. Like a well-spun novel, Evelyn couldn't wait to devour more. And she found herself rationing out the pages each day in order to prolong reaching the end. This was the real irony of the process. In the reading, Evelyn found herself forgetting that she already knew the end. She'd lived it too. Yet despite the pain that lay ahead, she was savoring the journey.

Why was that? The quality of writing explained a portion of the intrigue, but it was more than that. Evelyn tried to put her finger on it by recalling the scenes she had read.

Nell's description of their means of transportation to California was so apt—the first truck off Henry Ford's assembly line with a Conostoga wagon in tow. They'd brought along only the barest necessities for furnishings, yet the tarped wooden trailer seemed full to brimming. And the flat tire that it sustained in the middle of Utah had been absolutely devastating. Evelyn could still recall the heat, the perspiration, the utter desolation that she'd felt as they unloaded it. But Nell had smiled and made jokes the entire time.

"Just think, Evelyn. This is what the pioneers must have endured when they broke a wagon wheel. At least we don't have to worry about the Indians."

Just then an approaching cloud of exhaust heralded a vehicle. The red Chevrolet pickup clamored to a halt behind their broken conveyance, and a tall dark man of obvious Native American ancestry stepped out.

Edward, Evelyn, and Nell stopped their work and stared, dumbfounded.

Finally he raised his arm in greeting, palm outward. "How," he said and smiled.

"How else?" Nell responded, tongue in cheek, before collapsing in a fit of laughter.

The man, Sam Lonewolf, gave Edward and their damaged tire a ride to the nearest town. Then he returned them both, along with sandwiches and sodas, and assisted Edward in replacing the repaired tire. Nell insisted that they have a picnic lunch around the kitchen table in the ditch.

Oh, that had been a wonderful time. Funny, but Evelyn had forgotten all about it, while Nell had even remembered the man's name. Of course she'd probably recorded it in her diary shortly after the occurrence. The details, however, were far more vivid than Evelyn would have written them. Nell seemed to note so many of the small things in life.

That was it, Evelyn realized. While she had been bemoaning their bad luck, anxious only to reach their destination, Nell had been relishing the details of the journey. In fact, she treated all of the events in her diary in that manner. Evelyn suddenly understood that this was the same way that Nell had approached life in general—savoring the little incidentals along the way.

Once they'd reached San Francisco, they found two apartments in the same building on the second day—minimal one-bedrooms, but affordable. Edward had already arranged to work with a friend in his home construction business, and he began his new job as soon as they moved in.

Nell, on the other hand, had chosen to fly by the seat of her pants for a while. Her teaching certification was useless in California anyway, and she had some money saved up. For a month, she and Evelyn had a grand time together—sewing curtains for their dowdy apartments, picking up household odds and ends at garage sales, and of course, seeing the sites.

Evelyn remembered feeling chagrined to think that she'd been envious of having Nell accompany them. San Francisco had sounded like an oasis in which she and Edward could start all over again. Illogical as it sounded, she'd believed the change of scenery and the forced togetherness would conspire to create the child that had thus far eluded them. So when Nell finagled the invitation to come with, Evelyn felt almost betrayed.

But the city wasn't the haven she'd imagined. To Evelyn, who had only lived in Crow River, it was a foreign, impersonal landscape—fraught with crime and neighbors who wouldn't even say hello.

Nell's spirit, however, had never burned brighter. Her personality thrived on the excitement. The unfriendly neighbors provided a challenge that she easily overcame. Within three weeks of her arrival, she knew them all by name, and they knew her as well. It wasn't a bit surprising that she was offered a job at the neighborhood library. She accepted and began working exactly one month to the day after they had first set foot in the city.

Evelyn shuddered beneath the blanket. She realized now that Nell's job had been the beginning of a downward spiral for both of them. Yet even as she dreaded to read further in the diary, she knew that she'd pick it up again. But not tomorrow. Tomorrow was Mother's Day.

The next morning during church, Evelyn sensed that Susan seemed to sit a bit stiffly beside her. She would've suspected that it had something to do with her recent birthday, if the two of them hadn't just spent such a pleasant evening together at the supper club.

Pastor Masterson, too, seemed to be suffering from anxiety of some type. His sermon was a little lifeless. He fumbled with the communion wafers that he placed in their palms. And he did an unusual thing—resting his hand on Susan's head while she knelt at the railing. Evelyn felt the tension radiating from her daughter with his gesture.

Evelyn shook his hand in the receiving line after the service. "Pastor," she said, scrutinizing his face, "what happened to your nose?" Three scratches swept downward.

"My, my," Susan spoke up behind her. "That *does* look nasty...almost as though you stuck it where it didn't belong."

He reddened. "Susan," he whispered. "I have *tried* to apologize. You simply won't give me the chan—"

"Wonderful sermon," her daughter interrupted. "But then I'm not surprised. You are terribly good at assumptions." With that remark, delivered with a smile, Susan grasped Evelyn's elbow and propelled her onward.

"What was *that* all about?" Evelyn asked on the outside steps.

"Nothing."

"Susan."

"Later. We'll discuss it later. The roast should be done."

The Sunday meal at Susan's house was as delicious as usual and executed in her customary formal manner—china dishes, cloth napkins, and a fresh floral centerpiece. Evelyn bet that she'd paid too much for the latter and wished again that her daughter would take up gardening.

"Would you like your pie now, Mom, or later?"

"Later, dear. Right now I'd like an explanation please."

Susan slumped back down in her chair. "Shoot. I thought you'd forget."

"Not a chance."

The startling chime of the doorbell intruded. Peanut leapt up from under the table and darted to the door, yapping. "Saved by the bell," Susan uttered with relief as she rose to answer.

"Please, Susan. Don't slam the door in my face again."

Was that Pastor Masterson's voice? Evelyn couldn't be sure with all the barking going on. She cautiously leaned in her chair to see around the dividing wall. The front door came into view. It *was* the pastor. She quickly ducked back, her brows knit in confusion.

"I haven't slept well for the past two nights. Would you please call off your dog?"

"Peanut, let's put you outside." The screen door creaked open, then shut again on the muted barking. "Shh," Susan continued. "My mother's here. Please keep your voice down."

Evelyn crept backwards in her wheeled chair ever so quietly until she reached the separating wall. They were whispering now. Drat. She leaned her ear to it and was just able to discern the conversation.

"...and John explained everything to me."

"You told John?"

"I had to explain the scratches."

"You couldn't have just said that you got *down* on the wrong side of the bed?"

"Very funny. I'm miserable here. I realize that I shouldn't have jumped to conclusions, and I'm very ashamed of myself. Would you please forgive me, Susan?"

There was a lengthy pause while Evelyn held her breath.

"Oh...all right. I suppose telling John was punishment enough."

"Thank you." He sighed. "Wow. I feel *so* much better."

"It's forgotten." Raising her voice, she continued. "Mom, you can stop listening at the wall."

Evelyn shot up and smoothed her skirt. She stepped around the corner. "Are you going to tell me what this is all about?"

Susan crossed her arms and grinned. "Not a chance."

Pastor Masterson's face flushed.

Evelyn cleared her throat. It was obvious that she'd gleaned all the information she was going to get. "Pastor, we were just going to have some pie. Would you join us?"

"But I thought you wanted to wai—"

"Nonsense, Susan. We have company. Let's be hospitable." She turned to the pastor. "My daughter makes the *best* apple pie. You'll simply *have* to stay and try a piece." To Susan, she said, "What kind of apples do you use, dear?"

"Huh? Oh…Braeburn."

"Ah yes…Braeburn. I'll help you dish it up and put the coffee on."

Pastor opened the conversation as they were seated around the dining room table a short while later. "Mrs. Justison," he began as he picked up his fork, "I understand you like to read."

"Oh yes. I love to read."

"The public library contacted me this week and asked if I could suggest some volunteers for their new story hour program. Would you be interested?"

"What does it involve?"

"Reading aloud to children. Apparently they'll hold several daily sessions during the summer months and are hoping to line up several people to share the responsibility."

What a wonderful idea, Evelyn thought. She ran her fingertip along the rim of her coffee cup. She had so enjoyed reading to Susan when she'd been a little girl. There was nothing better to inspire children to become avid adult readers. But did she want the added task each day? "Could I think about it and let you know?"

"Absolutely. Just give me a call either way by the end of the week." He turned to Susan, extracting an envelope from his inside jacket pocket. "I almost forgot. Kimberly asked me to give this to you."

Susan took it from his proffered hand. She loosened the seal and pulled a card from within. Her face showed confusion as she silently read the verse. "It...it's a Mother's Day card. I don't understand."

"Is it?" He leaned over and read it himself. "It says, 'Happy Mother's Day to a friend.' I hope you're not offended, Susan. I know she meant well. She's very fond of you."

Susan stared down at the colorful card in her hands. Her voice sounded ripe with emotion. "I...I'm not offended at all. Tell her *thank you* from me. T...tell her it's very special."

"Did she write something inside too? May I read it?"

She passed it to him, still staring downward.

He read aloud. "'I don't have a mother, but you're the next best thing. Thank you for teaching me everything.'"

Evelyn was touched. "That's beautiful. What did you teach Kim, dear?"

She swiped her eyes, gazed up with a smile, and shrugged. "Nothing much. I helped her get started with a little cooking, explained a little about cleaning and laundry. No big deal really. She's such a fast learner."

"Ah...," Pastor said. "So you're the one."

She glanced his way with narrowed eyes. "*The one* what?"

"The one who's been giving her recipes to use."

"Yeah. What's wrong with them?"

"Nothing...nothing. They're just a little...hot."

"You don't like *hot*?"

"Well, it gives me heartburn, that's all."

"Heartburn?" She leaned closer, waving her finger. "I'll have you know that *hot* cures what ails you."

"That's ridiculous. Where did you hear that?"

Evelyn cleared her throat. "Actually, I passed that on to her. Maybe it's just an old wives tale, but that's what my mother told me."

He reddened. "My apologies."

She waved her hand. "No need to apologize. As I said, it's probably just an old wives tale."

He shrugged. "Most wives tales *are* founded on truth in some way."

"Oh, look!" Susan exclaimed, reaching inside the envelope. "There's something else here." She removed a folded piece of notebook paper and opened it. A twenty-dollar bill fluttered to the floor. She bent to retrieve it and then read aloud. "'Susan, I want to give you this money to show you my appreciation for all you've taught me. And I also have a selfish reason too. I was wondering if you wouldn't mind using it to take Dad out for dinner tonight. I want to take Mother's Day off. Your friend, Kim.'" Susan glanced up with a hesitant expression.

Evelyn gazed from one to the other. Eric ran his finger inside his cleric's collar in a gesture of discomfort. "Well," she said to ease the tension, "it looks like you won't have to worry about hot food tonight, Pastor."

He upended his palms, imploring her daughter. "I'm sorry. I know this kind of puts you in an awkward situation. I'm sure Kim would understand if I told her we'd decided to take a rain check."

"Nonsense," Susan answered, regaining her composure. "The girl deserves to put up her feet tonight. The least we can do is give her the chance."

"But...I wouldn't want people to think—"

"Me either. We'll have to go out of town."

He considered that for a moment. "That'll work."

She sighed heavily. "Good. Okay. It's settled then."

Evelyn smiled to herself later as she drove home. She knew why. It was hope. Ridiculous. Very likely unfounded. But hope, nevertheless. Stranger things must've happened at some point in the history of the world. A minister and a carpenter. Suddenly she laughed aloud at her analogy and almost missed the stop sign at St. Paul Street.

But she'd have to be terribly careful, she cautioned herself the next moment. She'd had hope before and gotten carried away by it. No, it was important that hope always be grounded a bit with reality. If she didn't keep that in mind this time, the disappointment might be too devastating.

Wouldn't it be wonderful though, if Susan were to marry the pastor? What peace she'd feel if she came to die with the knowledge that her Susan wasn't alone.

Chapter 14

Susan couldn't have had poorer timing, despite the fact that she was punctual in picking up Eric for dinner. Debra Culpepper had arrived on his doorstep a few minutes earlier, a hotdish in hand that wreaked of oysters.

"What in the world—?" she began, watching Susan get out of her pickup and approach them.

"Ah...Susan and I were going to—"

"...see if John is home." Susan completed his sentence as she climbed the stairs. She smiled. "Ready to go?"

Debra took the hint, though she looked a bit confused, and he and Susan were underway a moment later. "Where are you going?" he asked as she turned down Darwin Street.

She grinned. "We're going to see if John's home, just like I said."

He wanted to say something—tell her she could take care of business with his brother some other time. The fewer people that knew about this *dinner together thing* that Kim had instigated, the better. Innocent as it was, the town was small and tongues would wag.

His brother's apartment building came into view. Susan glanced toward the parking lot and spotted the Mustang. "Yep. Looks like he's home." She drove right past it.

"But I thought you were going to—" Suddenly he understood. "Ah...I see. The ruse you told Miss Culpepper. You didn't want to lie."

"You got it."

Susan took them to a small restaurant that stood alone in the rural countryside, ten miles south of town. Like a beacon, its illuminated marquee along the state highway flashed the promise "Good Food." She explained that she often took prospective clients there to discuss their purchasing, selling, or remodeling expectations, so no one would draw any unjustified conclusions.

He pointed out that, since he lived in the church-owned parsonage, such a pretense might raise red flags.

"Then you can say that we're here to discuss my possible nomination to the church property committee or something like that," she suggested.

"Since you prefer not to lie, can I assume that you'd honestly accept such an appointment?"

She considered that a moment after turning off the pickup. "Yes," she decided. "I think I would. The truth is, that parsonage you're living in is in need of some serious renovations and updating. I'm surprised they haven't considered it before."

"Oh, they have, but finding the available funds seems to be impossible."

"Then they should sell it."

Now that was a viable alternative that he'd considered suggesting to the council on more than one occasion. There were many parishes now that no longer supported a parsonage for their clergy. Instead they provided a monthly housing stipend, leaving the choice of owning or renting a home entirely up to the pastor. Eric had to admit that he found the idea appealing. It seemed to make good investment sense for a pastor to own his own property when he reached retirement age. "So if you were on the property committee," he teased, "you'd vote to oust me from my home?"

She caught the gleam in his eyes. "Absolutely."

"Good. Then we'll have something legitimate to discuss at dinner."

They were seated in the cozy back room with no fellow diners. Eric ordered a rib-eye steak, medium, and Susan ordered a hamburger with fried onions. Conversation during the short wait for their meals was lively and comfortable. Eric found himself relaxing and thoroughly enjoying the company. Susan was serious about joining the committee. Their ideas for the fate of the parsonage were eye to eye, and he was convinced that her enthusiasm would carry the other members.

The waitress delivered their steaming plates and departed. "I can see where this would be a good thing for you too, Susan. You'd very likely get to list the parsonage, and there's a very good chance I'd have to avail of your agency's services in order to find a place of my own. Very shrewd."

She set her hamburger down and wiped her fingers on her napkin. "Thank you. I thought so." Indicating his plate, she said, "Try your steak."

He cut off a corner and slipped the succulent piece into his mouth—chewing, savoring, and swallowing. "Delicious."

"Better than oysters?" Her mouth quirked in a sly smile.

He grinned. "I hate oysters."

"Here, here. Good for you. But don't you think you should tell Miss *Dull*pepper?"

"What did you call her?"

"Oops. Was that out loud? Sorry."

Eric couldn't contain his wide smile. She wasn't sorry at all. But neither was she being spiteful. She'd simply thought of something clever to say, and she'd gone ahead and said it. How refreshing. People always minced words in his presence. To see a glimpse of someone's real personality, without an embarrassed apology, was very special.

"Are you supposed to be smiling like that?" she asked.

"No. Probably not. But it feels great."

"Good. That was my intention."

"Somehow I knew that." They smiled for a long while at each other with no awkwardness, no hidden motives—only two friends sharing each other's company. That was when he realized how thoroughly he'd been forgiven for his Friday night blunder. "John told me you just had a birthday."

"Yep. The big four-o."

"And how do you feel about that? Those decade birthdays can sometimes be hard to accept."

"I know what you mean. Thirty was tough for me. I think it was because I was unsure of where I was headed or something. It was like I thought I needed to stop and look at where I was and tally up how many of my goals in life were still unmet. It's funny, but I didn't feel the need to do that at all on this birthday."

"Why do you think that is?"

"Good question." She sighed heavily and stared long and hard into space. Then she gazed directly at him. "I think it's because I'm content right where I am right now. Oh, I still have some goals, but they're not all-consuming." She shrugged. "If they happen, they happen. If they don't, they don't."

He leaned closer, intrigued. "I know *exactly* what you mean. I feel the same way now, but it wasn't that way at thirty. Do you think it's because we're older and wiser?" She tipped her head, considering. He liked the way she gave the question serious thought. Marcus was the only other person he'd known who liked to speculate on psychological things like this.

"Yes." She nodded. "I think that's part of it. But a lot of people our age are still wrestling with their goals. I think it has more to do with your experiences along the way and what you learn from them. For example, when my dad died over five years ago, I was suddenly forced to face the fact that life was fleeting. I think I also learned that it can't be measured by what you acquire along the way, but by who you touch. Does that sound weird?"

Eric knew he was staring at her in a profound way, but what she'd just said *was* very profound. Not everyone who lost a loved one came to accept that perspective on life. Some became embittered or worked harder to stockpile the treasures that rust. "That's very profound, Susan. And very true. I reasoned through a similar crisis when my wife and…when my wife died." He paused uncomfortably, wanting to tell her about Kyle but afraid to do so.

"I understand. I think it's awful that it takes tragedies of one sort or another to get it through our thick skulls. We spend so many years chasing the wrong thing."

He swallowed, unable to look up from his plate and meet her eyes.

"Eric?" He forced himself to raise his gaze. Her brown eyes were shiny with tears. "Let's enjoy our meal, shall we?"

They did so, in companionable silence for some time. As though she sensed when he was again ready to talk, she asked, "Has John spoken to Marcy this weekend?"

"Yes. He called today to wish her a happy Mother's Day."

"And?" She waited. "C'mon. Spit it out. How did it go?"

He sighed. "I'm afraid she was a little terse and pulled her usual evasive tactic."

"She put the kids on?"

Eric nodded. "Yes. I don't understand it. She seems to be hiding behind the kids."

"She is." Her words were decisive. "Most likely, she has been for years. It's a common self-preservation strategy."

He stopped cutting his steak and stared at her. She nonchalantly dipped a French fry in catsup. It vanished into her mouth. "What are you talking about? Self-preservation from what?"

Susan stopped chewing, swallowed, and licked her fingers. She ran her napkin across her lips. "From emotional pain. From hurt."

"I don't understand."

"Marcy is starving for a little romance in her life. John thinks it's no longer necessary."

"He told you that?"

She fixed him with a condescending expression. "Of course not. He doesn't even know."

Eric rubbed his temple. "I'm afraid you've lost me. Did Marcy tell you that?"

"No. I've never met the woman."

"Then *where* are you getting this stuff?" He knew his voice sounded exasperated.

"Believe me, I know. I've seen it consistently happening to friends of mine. And John almost confirmed it to me on Friday night when he mentioned that you get to an age where all that mushy stuff is unnecessary."

"He said that?"

"Those weren't his exact words, but that was the gist of his opinion."

"So you told him what you suspected might be the problem. Right? You told him?"

She narrowed her eyes. "What right would I have to tell him that? I'm his employer, for heaven's sake. It wouldn't be appropriate."

"But you're positive that that's what the problem is between them?"

She nodded. "Absolutely."

He ran his fingers through his hair. "Why didn't you tell me this before? With the knowledge, I certainly could've mentioned it to him." She didn't respond. He glanced up to see her arms crossed on the table, her eyes just watching him. And he understood what she was communicating. How in the world would it have been appropriate to tell him about it? Almost the moment she'd arrived at her assessment, he had arrived at his assumption.

"I would have mentioned it earlier, but the time didn't seem right." He thought that was a very gracious way to word it. When Susan forgave, she obviously didn't rub a person's face in it afterwards. "But I've told you now, and I feel much better. Do you think John will be receptive to the idea?"

"He's one miserable guy, I'll tell you that. I think at this point, he'd be open to any idea. I've just got to figure out how to bring it up. I assume you'd like to remain nameless?"

"Yep. Nameless, faceless, totally out of the equation." They each thought quietly for a while. "How about if you were to draw on your own personal experience?" she finally suggested. "Like how important a little romance was to your wife?"

He scratched his chin. "I'll give it some thought."

As they were driving back later, however, Eric realized that he'd been giving all other matters no thought whatsoever. His mind, throughout the chit chat of the remainder of the meal, had been consumed with one thing—straining to find an example of romance from his own marriage. Oh, he found plenty of examples. But the problem was, they all dated back to their newlywed era. *BC*, he called it—*before children.*

Once Kyle and Kim had come along, their lives had become occupied with parenting. And it was good. They'd both loved being parents. They'd both been dedicated to the nurturing of their children to responsible adulthood—socially, intellectually, psychologically, and especially spiritually.

Sharon had been so wonderful with the church youth group. She'd had an open rapport with every one of the teens, including Kyle. That was a remarkable feat, when most kids considered it *not cool* to get along with their parents.

In fact, Eric was reminded again of how inadequate he had felt with their son. Weren't a father and a son meant to have a special bond? He'd always imagined that to be the case. It knifed him to think that he and his son had been the exception to the rule. The argument on the evening of the accident flooded his mind. He grasped his head to force it aside. Not now. Not now. It's over. It's done. We move on. God's forgiven me. Move on. Give me peace.

"Eric? Are you all right?"

He turned to see Susan at the steering wheel, staring at him with concern.

"Are you okay?" she asked again. He nodded. "We're here. You're home. Or should I say, 'You're back at the place that'll put some dough back in the church treasury'?"

How considerate she was—not asking any questions, trying to lighten the mood. "Is that right?" He managed a weak smile. "You sound pretty sure of yourself."

"Absolutely."

The cadence of the nighttime insects intruded on their comfortable silence. Eric didn't feel the need to rush inside. He should have. Hadn't he almost made a fool of himself? But Susan's response was so accepting, so nonjudgmental, that he wanted to rest in the feeling awhile longer. He leaned forward and peered upward through the windshield. "The stars are out. It's a clear night."

She was doing the same. "Mmm, hmm. Beautiful. I love the stars."

"Me too." They smiled at each other.

"I think—" She stopped mid-sentence and blushed.

"What do you think?"

"Oh, forget it. I don't know why I wanted to say it. I guess maybe just because I feel so comfortable, I thought I could."

"You can. Go ahead. Say it."

She took a deep breath and released it. "I was just going to say that I think some people think I'm weird because I never married."

"I don't think you're weird. But I admit that I'm curious as to why you never did."

"It's hard to explain. I guess it was just never a dream that I held. I've always been pretty independent. And I knew from a young age that I wanted to be in a business just like my dad. I guess I was always different from other girls that way. My visions of the future never included a guy to make them complete."

"You are who you are, Susan, and that's okay."

"That's what my aunt Nell used to tell me."

"Then she was a smart lady."

"Yeah. I always thought so. In fact, I always hoped I'd be a lot like her. But I guess the real reason that I brought it up is to remind you that most women do dream of getting married."

"I'm sorry. I don't follow you."

"Debra Culpepper."

"Ah...Debra. Yes. What was it you called her? *Dull*pepper?"

She blushed. "I didn't mean anything by it."

"I know."

"But believe me, I know that Debra is relentless. And if I'm reading you right, you're not interested. So I really think you need to tell her." He began to protest, but she waved it aside. "I know. You probably think it would be embarrassing, because she'll tell you that you're mistaken. But you are not mistaken. The proof is in the hotdish. So level with her, and if she says you're mistaken, so what? She has a right to save face however she needs to do it. Don't you think?"

It made perfect sense. He wondered why he'd never considered it in that light before. "You're absolutely right. I'll tell her tomorrow."

"Good." She beamed. "Because there's a new bachelor who's moving into town. In fact, he's closing on one of my houses tomorrow. And word has it...," she began with a wink, "he's very partial to oysters."

Eric laughed wholeheartedly and she joined him. As he said goodbye and exited the pickup, he turned back and extended his hand. She took it and shook. "Thanks for a great evening, Susan...the advice, the laughs, everything. I'm glad we're friends again."

"Me too."

He couldn't resist one final parting comment. What could he say? She'd put him in an unusual mood with her wit. "Besides, I wouldn't have lasted one more day as your enemy."

Chapter 15

▼

"Ah...Susan?"

She turned to face a very timid-looking John. He'd caught her just before she stepped up into her pickup after work on Thursday. "Yes? What's wrong?"

"Oh, nothing's wrong. In fact, everything's great. But I have a favor to ask."

"Okay, but I'll have to warn you. If it has to do with raises, bonuses, benefits, or vacation time, you'll only tick me off." She grinned to show she was teasing.

"What if it's about taking tomorrow off for a very important reason?"

"You're having major surgery? You have a communicable disease? You're dying?"

Smiling, he shook his head after each question.

"Ah, then you must think I'll give you a day off for foolish self-indulgence."

"Sort of. Marcy's flying in tonight."

"She is?" Susan knew her expression radiated her happiness. She couldn't resist giving him a hug too. "That's absolutely great, John. By all means, take the day off."

"Thanks. Things aren't patched up completely, but it's looking promising."

"I'm so glad to hear that, even if I'll be losing the best carpenter I've ever had."

"Hey, don't write me off the payroll yet. That's one of the things we'll be discussing—starting over. And I'd like to do it right here in Crow River. We'll see how she feels about it."

"What will you do if she doesn't like the idea?"

"Head back to Chicago." He said the words with no hesitation or regret whatsoever. Clearly, Marcy's wishes took precedence over his own. He'd realized what was most important in life.

Susan expressed her understanding. She suggested that he and Marcy might like to attend the Fireman's Fling on Saturday. There was a craft fair in the afternoon, followed by a chicken dinner and a big dance. It would be a good chance for Marcy to meet some of his friends since most of the town attended. After another brief and sincere hug, she wished him the best on his reunion with his wife.

When she arrived home for the evening, she tended to Peanut and Princess and then phoned her mother. Her talk of the Fireman's Fling had reminded her that she hadn't firmed up her own plans in that regard. "Mom? How's it going for you?"

"Quite well, dear. You'll think I'm silly, but I told Pastor he could put me on that volunteer list for the reading program."

"That's not silly at all. I think it's a great idea. You'll enjoy it."

"I hope so. But nothing ventured, nothing gained, I guess."

"Yep. Say, I was wondering if you were willing to venture the Fireman's Fling again with me this year?"

"I'd love to…but just the craft fair and the dinner. That dance gets too late, and I'm not getting any younger you know."

"Okay. Whatever you like, I guess. But I wish you'd go to the dance for a little while. I could bring you home and then go back myself alone."

There was a short hesitation. "I just don't know, Susan. I'll keep the offer in mind, but I'm sure the earlier activities will wear on me enough."

She teased her. "Can't get a man, Mom, if you don't flaunt your stuff at the dance."

"Susan! Honestly, you're terrible."

"I'm just teasing."

"I know, dear. But I'm well beyond flaunting anything, and I'm certainly not interested in a man."

"That makes two of us. See what a great pair we make?"

Her mom laughed. "Susan, you are the sweetest daughter any mother could have. I can't tell you how many times I've asked myself how I got so lucky."

"Sheesh, Mom. Enough. What's with all this sentimentality?"

Another lengthy pause ensued. "Just some reminiscing that I've been doing, dear. No big deal."

On Saturday afternoon, Susan and her mother enjoyed browsing the displays and visiting with friends and acquaintances. Cindy Gunderson had acquired a hand-hewn pine cabinet for her daughter's kitchen. "It will be so nice for them to put the microwave on," she explained. "I wanted to buy the matching wall spice rack, but Gary said enough was enough."

"Where is it?" Susan asked. "I'd like to buy it for a wedding gift for them."

"Oh Susan. Thanks. That would be great. It's over in the far corner. You'll recognize it. He has all sorts of beautiful handcrafted wood products."

She found the vendor and purchased the spice rack. They browsed around some more, and her mother debated on purchasing a set of embroidered dishtowels. "This will be a nice gift for Cindy's daughter and her husband," she said, "but I hate to buy them. I could so easily do it myself. I'm just concerned about finding the time now, what with the library commitment and all."

"Do it, Mom. It's a lovely gift whether you did the embroidery or not. And you might as well avoid the stress if you're concerned about your time."

Her mother purchased them and seemed relieved and satisfied with her decision. At four o'clock the vendors packed up their wares. And by five o'clock, the civic arena had been set with a long buffet table of mouth-watering chicken, mashed potatoes, gravy, vegetables, apple cobbler, and a salad bar that sported a generous variety of selections.

"Oh, look," her mom said when they'd reached the end with their fully laden trays. "There's Kim, the pastor, his brother, and that must be John's wife with them. I'd like to meet her."

"Then let's head over. It looks like there's room to sit by them."

Rows of tables were spread with plastic tablecloths and lined up end to end, up and down the lengthy span. They maneuvered their way down the appropriate aisle and were greeted warmly.

Marcy Masterson had beautiful shoulder-length red hair, fair skin, and blue eyes that were accentuated by her tasteful makeup. She exuded polish and class. Susan might've felt a little intimidated, had she not been so friendly.

"So you're Susan," she said with a sincere smile. "Kim has mentioned you several times. I'm so glad we got a chance to meet." She indicated the vacant chairs beside her. "Why don't you and your mom sit right here so we can talk?"

There were some people who you could talk to for hours and learn nothing about. But Marcy was genuine, down-to-earth, and frank. And she was as interested in learning about them, as they were about her. Susan thought she'd make a wonderful asset to Crow River and would fit in immediately. Of course she couldn't voice as much. Who knew if John had even broached the subject yet?

"I understand you have a career outside the home?" Susan prompted her.

"Yes, I do. Actually I'm self-employed now. My specialty is interior design."

Susan was intrigued. At one time, interior design had only been a viable business in a major metropolitan area, where the wealthy would avail of the service. But that was no longer the case. A remodeling competitor in a neighboring town had recently boasted in his flyers that his business included an interior design consultant. From all reports, the specialty had made a lucrative addition to his business. Apparently the new trend was now in demand even in the rural locale. "Do you work with corporate clients or the private homeowner?"

"Corporate. The money's good, but the games are nauseating."

"What do you mean?"

"The chain of command. My initial consultation will be with one person. By the time I've drawn up a proposal, someone else will be in the picture. By a third meeting, two others have joined the group. They seem to have committees for everything, but no one has the balls to make a decision." She covered her mouth in embarrassment. "Oops. Did I really say the 'B' word?"

Susan laughed with glee. "Yes, you did. Don't worry. No offense taken here. At least you have the 'B' to speak your mind."

Marcy's laugh was melodious. Her blue eyes sparkled with the familiarity of sensing a kindred spirit.

"Have you ever considered taking private clients…homeowners?"

"Have I ever. But the competition's just too fierce in Chicago. Even in the burbs, someone has already beaten me to the punch and established a name for themselves. It's an uphill battle."

Susan noticed John on the other side of Marcy, attentively listening to their conversation. They shared a significant look, and he raised a brow and then winked. Message noted, she thought, trying to contain the satisfaction that threatened to spill out in a smile. He knew what tack he could take with his approach. "Are you two staying for the dance?" she asked.

"We sure are," Marcy responded. "John has no choice. It's been a long time since he's taken me dancing." She turned and smiled at him, love shining in her eyes. He returned the gaze.

Susan smiled to see it. "I should warn you then. It's not rock and roll. It's polkas, waltzes, schottisches,—"

"Old time?" Marcy interrupted, wide-eyed with surprise. "Great! We love it!"

"Speak for yourself," John teased her.

"Oh, you are so full of it, John." She grinned at him. "You are the smoothest old-time dancer, and you know it. You're just embarrassed to admit how much you like it."

"Nope," he insisted. "I'd have to be a fool to be embarrassed to admit to something that I was good at. Wouldn't you agree?"

"What?" she retorted. "Did I hear you right? Are you giving me permission to agree that you're a fool?"

John sighed and appealed to Susan. "See what I have to put up with?"

"Yep, I do," Susan offered in mock sympathy. "But just think, it keeps you on your old-time toes."

The meal was over all too soon and the arena set for the grand finale. The buffet table was taken down, the eating tables were pushed aside to clear the floor, and the band was set up at the south end.

Her mom yawned. "Is the offer still open to run me home, Susan?"

"Sure. Whenever you're ready."

Marcy leaned over. "Evelyn, you're not cutting out on us already?"

"I'm afraid so. It's been a big day."

"I understand. Eric was going to bring Kim home. Can he give you a lift too?"

"Why certainly. If it's not too much trouble."

As they prepared to leave, Kim gave Susan an enthusiastic hug. It still warmed her heart when she did that. "Goodbye, Susan." She pulled away. "Is it okay if I bike over tomorrow afternoon?"

"Absolutely."

The band had finished tuning up and had launched into their first set of waltzes by the time Eric returned. He took a seat next to his brother, across the table from Susan and Marcy. It didn't take long before John and Marcy were out on the floor. They were a fluid couple together. Susan imagined that if Marcy had been wearing a full skirt instead of blue jeans, it would be gracefully swirling about her legs.

She and Eric maintained a steady dialogue throughout the evening. They discussed further ideas for remodeling of the church, Kim's dedication to her newfound hobby of homemaking, and their mutual satisfaction in seeing John and Marcy so happy. Conversation even turned to deeper issues for a while like God and the purpose of humans in His plan. "You captured part of it the other night, Susan, when you said that we're to touch others. We're here to show God's love to them."

"I agree, but you can't preach to everyone you meet, Eric. Some people are driven further away by direct attacks like that."

He pressed his finger to his lips in thought. "Yes. I suppose that's true if their hearts are hardened."

"Oh, that sounds so biblical...*hearts hardened*."

"It is."

"I know it is. But what does it mean? They're bitter? They're arrogant? They're angry? They're agnostic, not caring at all?"

"It means all of those things."

"Right. But when you get right down to it, they're just hurting. Whether it's emotional pain or a protective indifference, it all boils down to hurt. They can be hurt by the injustice life deals them, hurt by well-meaning Christians who fail time and again because they're only human, even hurt by a God who they just don't believe loves them. Whether the thing they blame has caused it or not, they're hurting and they're lost."

"Hey, you guys." John's voice intruded as he returned to his chair. "You two are looking *way* too serious. Lighten up a little. Relax. Have some fun."

"We are having fun," Eric responded. "We're debating."

"Yeah? Well, debate this then, why don't you? Debate getting off your butts and taking a swing around the floor. Susan, did you know my brother here is better than I am?"

"At what? Getting off his butt?"

"Very funny. No…at dancing. He's just too chicken to try it."

"I am not chicken." Eric's face turned to a mask of boyish stubbornness. Susan couldn't help smiling.

"Then prove it, bro." The gauntlet was set.

"C'mon, Susan." Eric rose, both from the table and to the bait.

They walked side by side to the center of the floor where he faced her, offering his left hand to her right. She placed her hand in his, and they began to move in effortless harmony. He *was* a good dancer, holding her not too close and guiding her by gentle pressure at her waist. Her left hand rested on his firm shoulder, and she felt thoroughly comfortable and unthreatened.

"Looks like Miss *Dull*pepper is enjoying herself," he said, indicating a couple to his left. "I assume that's *Oysterman*?"

Susan glanced in that direction and laughed. "You'd be correct. Doesn't look like she took too long pining over you before she made her move."

"I let her down easily."

She gazed up into his face. It held a childish expression of teasing. "Is that right?"

He gave a firm nod. "Absolutely." Then his face lit in a boyish grin.

Susan was captivated, lost in the magic of that charming innocence. Her own expression sobered in wonder of it all and their eyes held, silently communicating something. The laughter in his faded and was slowly replaced by an emotion she couldn't put her finger on. Not passion—hardly as threatening as that—but frightening all the same. What was it?

The moment passed, stripping away the fear it had induced just as quickly. The waltz ended. They companionably returned to the table. But Susan couldn't shake the memory of her confusion. What *was* that emotion she'd glimpsed in Eric's eyes?

Marcy and John applauded their performance. The brothers slipped into an easy conversation about cars, and Marcy lightly touched Susan's hand beneath the table. She searched her face. "He's hurting,"

Marcy whispered, nodding ever so slightly toward her brother-in-law, "because of Kyle."

Susan raised a brow and nodded as though she understood. But all she understood was what she'd witnessed a moment earlier on Eric's face. It was pain, utter anguish, and almost a plea for help. But long after she'd returned home, she couldn't shake the nagging confusion that had replaced the knowledge. She'd determined, almost intuitively, that Kyle must have been his son and that the pain must be related to the car accident that had claimed both his wife and his son. But for the life of her, she couldn't decipher why Eric had silently made his plea for help to her.

Chapter 16

▼

The peace and contentment that had hallmarked Evelyn's Sunday morning had been shattered by her ensuing visit with Hattie. After the service, two people casually remarked, "It was so nice to see the pastor dancing with Susan last night." Evelyn was elated with the news. In fact, she even detected something warmer in the pastor's brief handshake and a lingering in the gesture when he made it to Susan. Naturally, she hadn't asked her daughter for any specifics. To do so might put her on alert. And in some matters, it was far better for Susan to be blindsided.

A celebration seemed in order so she went to the nursing home directly afterwards. There she surprised her friend by taking her to the diner for a noon luncheon. And Hattie was her usual jovial self until she returned her to her room.

"Where's Adeline?" Evelyn asked. The neighboring bed was tightly tucked and made up, its slumbering occupant gone.

"She passed away during the night."

"Good heavens, Hattie! Why didn't you tell me?"

"Ah, you know me. I don't like to dwell on the sad when there's something better to think on. But I've got to tell you, Evie, your visit here today was a godsend. I could feel myself slipping into a funk."

Evelyn sat in the guest chair beside her and took her worn hand. "Why don't you talk about it? Sometimes it's good to let our feelings out."

And talk she did, but not about Adeline. Instead she reminisced about Nell. Nell, the person whose diary had been haunting Evelyn all week.

"We humans make a lot of mistakes in our lives," Hattie began, "and Nell was no different. The difference between Nell and Adeline though, is that I know Nell had come to terms with hers. Can't say the same about Addie...not 'cause she didn't, but because I don't know. She was never much interested in talking when she was awake."

Evelyn felt a shiver of foreboding race down her spine. "Ah...but Nell liked to talk? About the past, you say?"

"Not particularly. But it was all in her diaries."

She knew her gasp was audible. "You read her diaries?"

"Only two of 'em. She asked me to one time. Said it would make her feel better if I did." Hattie raised her brow. "Said she'd asked you too, but you never would. You really should, Evelyn. I think you need to if you're gonna make peace with the past."

She couldn't look into her face. "I...I am."

Hattie's hand came to rest on her knee and squeezed. "Good. And have you? Made peace?"

Evelyn gazed into her eyes. There was no condemnation there. "I'm trying to, but it's very hard. I...I just can't read any further. It's too difficult."

"You haven't finished yet?" she asked, surprised. Evelyn shook her head. "Then trust me, Evie. Keep reading and the peace will come."

Now Evelyn was ensconced in her recliner, the second diary in hand. But she couldn't bring herself to open it. How could Nell have aired all of their dirty laundry to someone else? They had sworn to each other that they'd never speak of it again—not between themselves. Certainly Nell had understood that the oath applied to anyone else as well.

Only one thought brought relief. The diary that she'd finished had made no mention of the bitterness she'd carried during that time. How could it? It was Nell's point of view, and Evelyn had never shared the reasons for her resentment. But in some ways, that fact didn't comfort her either. For in not explaining her reasons, Evelyn's behavior had seemed even more bizarre. That must have been how it had seemed to Nell too. Poor Nell. She must've been so confused by it.

"Evelyn," she'd called as she rapped on their door one evening after work. "Open up. I've just *got* to tell you about the funniest thing that happened at the library today."

The knocking continued but Evelyn ignored it. She was sulking in their small living room, and the last thing she needed was another upbeat report from Nell. Nell—the woman who was so charming that people would approach her, whether she initiated a conversation or not. Nell—the woman who could begin telling a story to one person and end up with an audience. Nell—who couldn't possibly understand how much it hurt to be denied a baby month after month.

"Evie? Is everything all right in there? Are *you* all right?" The pounding became fierce.

Guilt settled heavy on her heart. She hastily dried her eyes on her sweater sleeve and moved to the door, swinging it inward.

"My God, you look terrible, Evie. Are you sick?" Nell's hand reached out, touching her forehead. "Can I do anything for you?"

Evelyn just silently stared at her for a long while. Her perfect legs, in her perfect hose. Her chic skirt, blouse, and jacket. Her hair, twisted atop her head in the latest style. Her made-up eyes, wide with…worry. "I'd just like to be left alone, Nell. If you don't mind, please…please just leave me alone."

Nell stepped forward and wrapped her in a warm hug. "Ah…no baby again this month? I'm so sorry, honey. But it's not the end of the world. It'll happen sometime."

With all her strength, Evelyn shoved her back. "It *is* the end of the world…to *me*! Don't you *see*? Don't you *get* it? I've waited and waited, tried and tried. It will *not* happen *sometime*! I know it. I'm sure now. I've given up hope." She crumpled to the floor, crying, rocking with her arms wrapped around her knees. "Oh God...I've given up...I've given up. No hope...no hope."

"There, there, Evie. Let me hold you. I want to help you. I want to understand."

"Please...just...go away. Please...I'll be...all right. I just need...to be alone. I need...to think."

And when she heard Nell quietly turn and exit, closing the door behind her, Evelyn felt the most bitter hatred well up inside. Nell would *never* be able to understand why a baby was so important to her. How could she? Her life was full with friends, with work, with excitement, with freedom. Explaining her aching need to Nell would be like explaining to a millionaire why you only needed a puppy to make you the wealthiest person on earth.

Nell's visits became more infrequent and sometimes downright awkward. She never knew what mood she'd find Evelyn in and began to avoid their encounters. The close companionship they once shared was replaced by a polite superficial friendship.

Evelyn withdrew further and further, and not just from Nell. She began to exclude Edward as well, until he must've found himself feeling just as awkward in her presence as Nell did. She lost interest in even trying to make the child he so wanted, and he buried himself in his work to dull the pain. It was ironic that they never would've returned to Crow River with the financial security Edward acquired, if they hadn't endured that painful period. Yet Evelyn would've gladly struggled for the rest of their lives to make ends meet, if only she'd been spared that pain.

The second diary, that she still held unopened, would dredge up more pain—Nell's pain. For Edward wasn't the only one who was forced to escape. Nell, too, needed an anesthetic to Evelyn's indifference. And she found it in a man.

"Evelyn, I hate to bother you, but I really, really need to talk." Nell timidly crossed the threshold. "Can we sit down?" She indicated the table and they took chairs across from each other. "I...I don't know where to begin." She laughed once, uncomfortably. "I'm pregnant."

The world dropped out from under Evelyn. Nell, who couldn't be richer, would soon possess the one thing that Evelyn would almost sell her soul to obtain. "You're pregnant." The words were flat, like Evelyn's spirit. "You'll be getting married then."

"Ah...no." She took a fortifying breath. "You see...the father is already married."

She sat up straighter, piercing Nell with an incredulous stare. "Oh Nell. Don't tell me you got taken in by some dandy and—"

"No." The word hung in the air between them. "I knew. I knew all along." She began speaking faster, realizing that Evelyn's anger was barely contained. "It's not what you think. His intentions were honorable. You see, his wife had left him but—"

"Please, Nell. Spare me."

"But she came back and...and...it was very difficult, but he's decided to try again."

Evelyn shot up. "Even with his baby on the way? He'd leave you with his baby to go back to a wife who left him? Pleeeaaase, Nell. If you believe that, you're the most naïve—"

"He doesn't know."

She dropped back in the chair. "What?"

"It was all decided last week. I...I just found out about the baby today." She squared her shoulders. "I've decided that I will not tell him."

"You're going to raise the baby by yourself?"

"Yes. Yes I will."

"Do you know what people will say? What that child will have to endure in school? And you? Will you even be able to teach with the reputation you'll have earned?"

"Evelyn, please stop." The words were calm, but Nell's expression was pleading. "I've considered all of those things, and I'm more than willing to fight an uphill battle for the rest of my life for this child. I love it. And I love the father."

The tears that rolled down Nell's cheeks proved the truth of her claim. And they melted Evelyn's resistance. She moved around the table and took Nell in her arms, and they wept together for long minutes.

"Oh Evelyn. I've missed you so much. I feel so terrible coming to tell you this, but you're the best friend I've ever had. I didn't know where else to turn."

"There, there, Nell. It's all right."

"But it's *not* all right. You've wanted a baby for so long and haven't gotten one. I didn't plan one at all, and now I'm in an awful mess."

"It's not your fault that I can't have a baby. It's not your fault. It isn't. Quit blaming yourself."

Nell suddenly pulled away and looked her full in the face. "I love you, Evelyn. I do…so much. If you wanted my baby, I'd give it to you because I know you would be a better mother than I could ever be."

A knocking sound intruded. It took Evelyn a moment to realize that it was the present, pulling her from her memories. She shook her head to clear the fog and took in her surroundings. It was Sunday afternoon. The unopened diary was still in her lap. She placed it in the end table drawer and rose to answer the door. Pastor Masterson stood on the other side.

"I'm sorry to drop in on you, Mrs. Justison. Normally I prearrange parishioner home visits, but…well, this is a bit unusual and of a personal nature."

She forced herself to concentrate on hospitality. "That's quite all right, Pastor. Come right in. I was just relaxing in my easy chair and must have dozed off for a minute." She indicated the couch and he sat, while she took a seat in the wing-backed chair facing it. "Now, how can I help you?"

"Actually this feels kind of awkward. I don't even know how to begin."

She studied him for a moment. His fidgeting and reddened face seemed to make the possibility logical, and she felt that forbidden hope welling up within her again. "Just begin wherever you like, and I'm sure I'll be able to piece it together."

"Okay." He took a deep breath and released it. "It's Susan. I like her. I mean...I like her as a woman. I'd like to date her. I mean...I hope you wouldn't mind if I were to ask her out. It's kind of strange, being in this position, but I thought if I did...ask her out, and she accepted...well, it might make you feel a little uncomfortable since I'm your pastor."

Evelyn was smiling. He looked so boyish and embarrassed. "That would be just fine with me. I don't think I'd feel uncomfortable."

He exhaled a long breath and relaxed. "Good. I mean...I'm glad that you approve."

"There is one thing though, Pastor, that you might want to consider."

"What's that?"

"Susan might not be receptive."

His amicable expression sobered. "But we seem to get along well. We can talk about anything. I like the way she gives my questions honest thought, and...well, she's certainly not afraid to argue about something she disagrees with."

"That would be Susan all right. I know you get along well...as friends. She has many *friends*. I'm just cautioning you about mixing romance with it. I honestly don't know how she'd react. It's been so long since she had a dating relationship with anyone that I couldn't even guess as to how she'd feel about it."

"I don't understand that. She's a beautiful woman. She's intelligent. She's social. It's hard to believe someone hasn't claimed her by now."

"*That* would definitely be the wrong word to use around Susan—*claimed*."

He reddened. "I didn't mean it that way. I just meant it's surprising that she's still single."

"Yes. I understand. Let me tell you what I think part of the reason might be. This is only what I've pieced together from observation, mind you, so it's just a theory that I have."

He leaned closer, resting his elbows on his knees and listening attentively.

"Susan was very, very close to her aunt Nell, as you know. She idolized Nell from the time she was a child. Well, Nell had a bit of an embittered opinion about men for many years. I didn't notice that at all in her later years, but that wasn't the case when Susan was younger. I think it's possible that some of Nell's misguided opinions from that time might've rubbed off on Susan a bit."

He nodded his understanding. "Thank you, Mrs. Justison," he said as he rose. "I'll certainly keep that in mind."

"But unspoken." She smiled.

"Yes, it will remain unspoken."

They shook hands warmly. Evelyn considered offering him a hug but discarded the idea. That would be too premature. She watched the bounce in his step as he walked to his car. Happiness and hope swept over her for a moment.

Evelyn suddenly felt exhausted. And it was no wonder. She'd been on an emotional roller coaster all day. It would probably be best to lie down for a while and have a nice nap. She wondered if she could consciously will away any bad dreams and replace them with only the good. Nell used to talk in the later years about the circle of life. Evelyn took it to mean "everything that comes around, goes around." There was no doubt that Evelyn had been traveling the circle of the past too much recently. As she drifted to sleep, she wondered if it were possible to bisect the circle on the inside, like a shortcut to the other side. Could a person skip past the pain and just cut across to the pleasure? Maybe one could, in death. Maybe that's what death was like. But certainly not in life. Life was pain and pleasure, with the former enhancing the latter. Or was it the other way around? No, that didn't seem right. Before she could analyze it further, she faded into slumber.

Chapter 17

"Hey, anybody home?" Marcus called through the screen door.

"Yeah," Eric responded, "but I'm on my way out. C'mon in." He took a final inspection in the bathroom mirror, checked the smoothness of his face, and exited through the open doorway.

"Well, look at you." Marcus grinned, then stepped closer and sniffed. "What's that I smell?"

"Aftershave."

"Aftershave? At 7:00 in the evening? If I didn't know better, I'd think you had a date." Eric felt his face flush. "Nooo. Really?"

"I'm hopeful."

"With who?"

"Miss Justison."

"Miss Justison? You mean Susan? Wow, Eric, I don't know what to say. I mean I'm happy you've changed your mind about...well, you know, about the whole subject. But I think you picked a real challenge."

"Yeah. Her mother kind of warned me about the same thing."

"You spoke to her mother? Man, you really *are* serious, aren't you?"

"I don't know how to explain it, but we seem to understand each other."

"Hey Eric, that's great." He clasped him on the shoulder and released it. "So she's expecting you then?"

"No. I just thought I'd drop over and suggest a drive."

"Well, good luck. Say, where's Kim?"

"Up in her room. Call her down if you like."

"I think I will. We could play *old maid* or something." He grinned devilishly. "Or is that only *your* game now?" Eric punched his arm. "Hey, hey, I was just kidding."

"I know. But just so you can't say I didn't warn you, I think Kim will want to play poker. Susan just taught her how."

The blood drained from his friend's face. "God help us."

He grinned. "Amen to that."

A short while later, Eric stood nervously on Susan's front doorstep. He cleared his throat and pushed the bell. Excited yiping sounded from the back of the house and grew more ear shattering as it approached.

The inner door opened. Susan's head appeared, wrapped in a pink towel. "Down Peanut. Get down! Here, let's put you outside." The screen door swung open. Peanut spilled out, attaching himself to Eric's leg. "Hello, Eric. Down Peanut! Down! Bad boy! Bad! You'd better get inside while he's distracted."

"Me or the dog?"

"Very funny." When he'd slipped safely in, she asked, "What brings you over? Something about the committee?"

"Ah...no. I thought maybe you'd like to go for a drive."

"A drive?" Her face changed from confusion to wariness. "What for?"

"I'd just like to talk for a while. And it's such a beautiful evening, I thought a drive would be nice." He grinned. "We could stop at the Dairy Queen."

"Are you buying?" He nodded. "You're on." She started for the door.

"Aren't you going to take off your turban?"

"No. I thought it'd be fun to leave it on and see what people say. Sound good?"

He held his breath, speechless. A trick question. Great. He'd lose either way.

She laughed. "Just kidding. Man, you should've seen your face."

Eric smiled after her as she moved down the hallway to the bathroom. He loved her sense of humor. If only he were quicker that way himself. It would be fun to throw her off guard, shock her with something witty or clever. And the view of her from the back was worth smiling at too. In fact, he decided that she looked enticing from any angle. He closed his eyes for a moment thinking about the Song of Solomon and immediately decided that was a bad idea.

"Ready to go?"

His eyes shot open. She was staring at him quizzically. He could feel his face flush. "Yeah. All set."

"Were you praying or something?"

"Ah...no. Just thinking."

Eric considered opening the passenger door for her but then discarded the notion. His instincts told him such a gesture might annoy her or, at worst, bring her guard up. Best to proceed as platonic friends and test the waters.

Susan reached for the seatbelt and snapped it in the buckle. "You know, this Taurus doesn't really seem right for you."

"Really?" He buckled his own belt. "What would seem right for me?"

She grinned. "A Mustang."

"Don't I wish." He smiled back.

A lineup of people waited their turn at the outdoor window of the Dairy Queen. "It looks like you picked the wrong place for anonymity," she said as they took their place at the end.

"That's okay. People tend to think what they choose to anyway." And personally, he hoped they were all thinking that they were a couple. She didn't seem worried that they might, if her relaxed stance was any indication. That was a good sign. "What'll you have?" he asked when they finally reached the window.

"Hmm. I think I'll have a strawberry sundae, medium-sized."

He spoke to the teenager on the other side. "One medium strawberry sundae and one medium hot fudge please."

Susan whispered when the girl left to fill the order. "At least she didn't ask if it was *to go*."

He laughed. There were no other choices—not even a picnic table outside. He paid for the sundaes, and they took them to sit in the car.

"So you're a hot fudge guy, huh?"

"Yeah. I'm allergic to strawberries."

"Really? What else are you allergic to?"

He hated to admit it. "Cats."

"No kidding? That's funny. I have a cat and you haven't start sneezing or anything when you've been at my place."

"It's more like a stuffed up feeling and runny eyes, and it only happens after prolonged exposure."

"Oh, I see."

"You have ice cream on your cheek." Without thinking, he reached over and gently swiped it off, wiping it on his napkin.

She blushed. "I could've done that."

"You don't say?" He shrugged. "Much simpler this way though. I didn't have to feed you the coordinates of where to swipe."

She laughed. "That was great! You're pretty witty."

A warm feeling passed through him. He hoped she didn't notice.

"Where to now?" she asked when they'd finished and discarded their trash.

Eric was elated that she didn't assume he'd be bringing her right home. "How about a drive around the lake?"

"That sounds good."

They meandered slowly around the perimeter of Round Lake at the south edge of town. Homes were tucked along every square foot of shoreline on the west side. Susan pointed out a couple of houses that her company owned and told him about the renovations they'd made. When he reached the south side, he pulled into the county park and stopped on the edge overlooking the water. He shut off the key, snuffing the soft purr of the engine to silence. The sun was still visible through the dense trees in the west. Its rays had turned the glimmering surface to an iridescent pattern of light. They watched quietly for several moments.

It was so peaceful. Eric had always loved sunsets, and it had been so long since he'd shared one with someone else. Kyle had liked sunsets too. He wanted Susan to know that.

She spoke softly, staring straight ahead. "You're going to tell me what you wanted to tell me on Saturday night." Her head turned and their eyes met.

"I'd like to. The truth is, I've never told anyone here."

"Why me?" Her voice was the faintest whisper.

"Because you'd understand."

Susan nodded almost imperceptibly and seemed to take a fortifying breath.

"I had a son…Kyle. He would've been seventeen this August." Eric thought it would be difficult to begin, but it felt cleansing. How long had he refused to say his son's name out loud? How long had he pretended that he'd never existed? "I'm not sure why I've refused to tell people that."

"Because it would've been too painful for you."

"How could you know that?"

"I saw it in your eyes. I see it again now."

Eric didn't doubt it. He could feel it in his heart—squeezing, constricting, suffocating. "He…Kyle…was driving the car. The accident killed them both."

"Tell me what happened, Eric."

He told her about the sharp curve that Kyle had no business taking so fast. He'd only had his learner's permit for two months. "I've wondered many times if he'd seen me do something similar and was just trying to imitate it. I was supposed to be with him that night, but an emergency meeting came up at church. Sharon went with instead." He laughed bitterly. "Some emergency meeting. It was the cemetery board…some tax matter that had to be resolved. And three days later I was burying my family because of a cemetery board meeting."

Eric took a deep, shuddering breath before he could continue. "Kyle was so angry at me before they left. We hadn't been getting along very well. This time he was angry because I'd promised to take him out to practice his driving. He was right though. I *had* promised."

"But things often come up that we can't foresee. Kids that age have trouble understanding that."

"I know, but he had a right to be mad. It hadn't been the first time. My parish was much larger than this one. The assistant pastor had left, and I was trying to do it all for a while. It was very hard for me to set the right priorities back then. Not so anymore. Whenever Kim needs me, I'm there."

"It shook up your faith, didn't it…the accident, the what ifs, the whys?"

"Ohhh yes. I was just going through the motions for a long time…empty, disillusioned, lost."

"How did you get it back?"

"Tough question." He sighed. "It's hard to explain. I guess it began with this fleeting glimpse of eternity. I don't mean I saw it. I mean it was more like this *sense* of its reality. It was only for a second that I felt that way. But I kept concentrating on the idea…on the reality of it, whenever I'd be in the most danger of falling apart. And very gradually, I found myself regaining my hope and my faith." Susan nodded her head. She understood. She grasped it. But he'd known she would. "Now you're probably wondering why I never told anyone else."

"Yes. Why?"

"I didn't want the sympathy, the fawning."

"Because you didn't feel you deserved it."

"Why would you come to that conclusion?"

"Eric…the pain. Remember? I saw it. I even see it now. You've accepted what happened. You've even accepted God's forgiveness for any fault you might have played in it. But you've never forgiven yourself."

He turned away from her and stared out the windshield. Nightfall had come. The water was black, save the gleam from the streetlight near the car. Was that it? Had his inability to forgive himself made it so difficult to accept sympathy? It made sense.

Eric recalled when Kyle had been small, the two of them used to take walks together in a park near home. There was a small pond in the center. One night they were out later than usual, and the water looked just like Round Lake did now—black and forlorn. Kyle clung to him when a frog made a sudden splash in the water. "Don't worry, Kyle," he told him. "I'll protect you." That's what a father did. He protected his children and made them feel safe. And in one night, Eric had failed miserably at his most important job.

"Have you forgiven Kyle?"

"For what?"

"For driving recklessly that night. For allowing his anger to get out of hand. For acting so irresponsibly that he killed himself and your wife."

Eric turned to gape at her in shock. How could such heartless words have come from her mouth? But they had. "It wasn't intentional," he snapped. "He didn't know that his actions would result in a car accident." He shook his head. "I can't believe that you'd say that...that you'd blame him."

Susan stared unblinkingly, no remorse in her eyes. "So you've forgiven him then."

"Of course I've forgiven him. There was nothing to forgive." The silence was heavy, her stare unrelenting. It seemed to touch something deep in his soul.

Still boring into him with her eyes, she spoke. "And why are you so different, Eric? Did *you* know that the harsh words you exchanged would force Kyle to drive so recklessly? Does your position as a parent or someone older or even a man of God, endow you with godlike characteristics of clairvoyance? Did you intentionally lash out at him in order to leave him no choice but to drive that way?"

"Of course not." He closed his eyes on the excruciating pain. "I just wanted him to understand the pressure I was under."

Her warm hand softly touched his. He opened his eyes to see his pain in her own. "Then what's there to forgive yourself for?" she whispered.

Suddenly it became so clear that he wondered why it had escaped him before. He'd acted as any father under stress might have acted. He'd acted out of his humanness. To deny that humanness would be to set himself as superior to God, wouldn't it? There was nothing to forgive but his human frailty, and God had already done that.

Eric reached across the seat and wrapped Susan in his arms for the sheer elation that he felt at the discovery. It was cleansing. It was freeing. And he wanted to share the pure joy of it with the person who'd made him see the truth. Her petal soft cheek rested against his. He turned his head and touched his lips there reverently. She smelled so fragrant. She felt so fragile. "I love you," he breathed.

Susan stiffened and he instantly pulled away. With one look at her stark face, he knew that he'd said the wrong thing.

Chapter 18

▼

So many thoughts tumbled through Susan's head. The foremost one was that she wanted to go home where she could be alone to process the rest. She liked Eric. He was a wonderful friend. She felt comfortable with him. Never once had she felt threatened, worried that he might misread their relationship. But apparently he had. And she felt an overwhelming sense of loss. Nothing would ever be the same between them again.

"I won't say I'm sorry, Susan, for speaking from my heart. It just wasn't supposed to be out loud." He sighed.

Susan couldn't look at him for fear of what she might see—embarrassment, remorse, or love. Whatever emotion he showed her, it would only intensify her guilt. She was letting him down. But she was helpless to respond in any other way.

"I'll take you home."

The drive was heavy and silent until at last, he pulled into her driveway. Eric left the car idling and stepped out before she could protest. He walked around, opened her door, and waited gallantly while she exited. Then he fell into step beside her as she approached her door. She glanced his way in confusion.

"It was a date. I didn't tell you that, but that's what it was. Probably the first and the last, but I want it to end properly."

She gained the top step and turned to say *goodbye* or something else that might be suitable. Eric was gazing at her with the most tender expression she'd ever seen. Her heart skipped a beat and then seemed to dissolve.

"Nothing has changed between us, Susan, except that I've recognized how I feel about you. We're still friends. We're still fellow debaters. All I want is a chance to see if you might come to feel the same way." His beautiful face was solemn, his blue eyes intense. "Will you give me that chance?"

She saw hope in his expression and felt powerless to strip it from him. "But what if I don't...come to feel the same? Don't you see that would risk everything we have now? I couldn't bear for that to happen."

Eric's brow rose. "Then perhaps that would be a good place to start. Maybe you need to ask yourself why that would cause you such pain."

She stood mesmerized as he closed the small distance between them. Like a slow motion film, his fingertip gently traced her jaw. She closed her eyes to savor the tingling sensation that such a small gesture evoked. It spread from her face to every nerve ending.

"Susan."

The breath of her name as Eric murmured it, whispered across her lips. Then she tasted it on his mouth as he skimmed hers with his own. His soft teasing seared her with a thirst for more. She mimicked his kisses, softly sweeping her lips back and forth, back and forth.

"More," he breathed.

Their mouths sealed. Their tongues touched and glided in a heady, lingering ballet. Susan knew she was lost and drowning in her senses, but she didn't care. She had never been affected this strongly by a kiss.

Eric brought them both to the surface slowly. "You're so beautiful, Susan. Such passion." He cupped her face and stared into her eyes. "May I call you tomorrow?"

She nodded. No other response was possible, so swamped were her emotions.

"Okay. I'll call you then."

Susan snuggled into her bed later, surprised to discover that she didn't want to sleep. Normally she welcomed slumber, especially on a Sunday night when the entire busy workweek loomed before her. As Princess shaped her nest beside her, Susan turned and scooped her cat's purring body up close against her own. Then she realized why she fought unconsciousness. She was savoring every moment of Eric's kiss. And in the back of her mind as she faded out, was the fear that the morning light would strip it of its magic. But she awoke with the memory just as vivid. In fact, the spell was even more enchanting in the pink light of a new sunrise.

John pulled her aside as soon as he arrived at work to tell her that Marcy had agreed to make the move. "She figures it'll take her about six months to finish up with her current clients," he explained. "We'll put the house on the market as soon as I get back there."

"That's great, John. I'm so happy for your both."

"That's it? 'That's great, John. I'm happy for you.'" He tipped his head, studying her in confusion. "Aren't you wondering when I'm leaving for Chicago?"

"Oh yeah. When are you leaving?"

"By the end of the week."

"Okay. That sounds good. Keep in touch, so I'll have an idea when you'll be coming back."

"Susan, what's wrong with you?"

"Huh? Nothing. Why?"

"Are you forgetting that we'll be in touch a lot, since you'll be looking for a place for us here?"

She reddened. "Oops. You're right. I *did* forget. Silly of me. Guess I'm not myself today."

That was a stupid explanation, she realized. But true. The rest of the workday crawled at a snail's pace despite her busyness. And she found herself constantly struggling in order to respond to questions coherently.

At six o'clock Eric called as she was sitting down to her dinner. His deep voice spread a smile across her face, warmth throughout her body. They talked about John and Marcy. They talked about what they'd each accomplished during the day. They talked about silly, incidental things like what they'd each eaten for lunch.

"I suppose I'd better let you go, so you can eat," he finally said.

Susan felt a keen disappointment. Couldn't they just go on talking all evening? She glanced at the clock and was stunned to see that they practically had. It was almost 8:00 p.m. Her cold and congealing dinner no longer looked appealing to her. But it was well-received by her pets.

Kim came to visit her on Tuesday evening. Susan didn't discern anything different in her behavior. Obviously she was still unaware of the new relationship that Susan had with her father. School was almost out, and Kim was concerned about finals. Susan reassured her that she'd do fine, knowing that Kim tended to over-study. Then she sent her home with another recipe that she'd modified to be less spicy.

Eric didn't phone until ten o'clock. Susan was reading in bed. His voice again sent skitters down her spine, but they were more acute. There was something terribly erotic about talking to him from her bed. And her reading material didn't help matters.

"What are you reading?" he asked through the earpiece.

She blushed. "Song of Solomon."

There was a pause and he cleared his throat. "Do you like it?"

"Very much."

"Me too, but I can't read it these days. It makes me miss you."

Susan could feel her heart pounding. "I miss you too."

"Would you like to go for ice cream and a drive tomorrow night?"

She smiled. "Yes."

The next evening, they again took a spot at the end of the long line. But this time Eric held her hand. She felt proud to stand beside him, knowing that people would recognize how they felt about each other.

"The usual?" he asked with a grin when they reached the window.

"No, I think I'll have hot fudge tonight." She had no idea how allergies worked but refused to take any chances. Her vision of the evening's end included a kiss. And she wouldn't be put off by any lingering traces of strawberries in her mouth.

Eric's bewildered gaze turned to understanding. "Hot fudge it is then."

When they took their ice creams to his car, Susan noticed several people from church for the first time. One of them greeted Eric as he held Susan's door open for her. "Good evening, Pastor."

"Hello, Mr. Oldenberg. Beautiful evening, isn't it?" He closed Susan's door and came around to the driver's side, handing her his treat and slipping his long frame beneath the steering wheel. "Thanks," he said as she passed it back to him. "Wish I could get that man to stay awake during my sermons."

"It's not you, Eric. Mr. Oldenberg has slept through every sermon since I was a little girl. I think it's amazing how straight he can keep his back."

"You would."

She glanced over to see him grinning from ear to ear with a splotch of fudge on his lip. Without thinking, she leaned over and swiped it off with her tongue. She pulled back, feeling satisfied that she'd been able to do something so uninhibited.

His expression was stern. "You can't do something like that in a public place like this."

Humiliation swept through her, but she lashed out in anger. "Why not?"

"Susan." He emphasized her name as though he were speaking to a child. "I'm a *minister*."

"That's right. You're a minister. M-I-N-I-S-T-E-R. I think you're confusing your vocation with a priest. That's P-R-I-E—"

"I know how to spell it."

"Good, but do you know the difference? Unmarried ministers are allowed to date."

"I only meant that something like that shouldn't be done in such a public place. People could get the wrong idea and speculate on what we might be doing in private."

"So what? You said yourself that people believe what they choose. Would a short peck have been inappropriate? Because they could just as easily have interpreted my action to be a short peck."

"Why are you so angry?"

Susan turned aside so he couldn't see the tears that were welling up. "I'm not angry, Eric. I'm humiliated. I wish I could just disappear."

"Oh Susan. Honey, come here. I'm sorry. The last thing I wanted to do was embarrass you." He reached out to her.

She shrugged away. "Don't…please. People are watching. Just bring me home."

"But you haven't touched your ice cream. It's melting."

"Could you throw it away? I'm sorry, but I wouldn't be able to eat it anyway."

He took the dish from her hand and got out to discard it. When he slid back inside, he asked, "Are you sure you want me to bring you home so soon?"

No, she wanted to say. *I want to be with you every minute. I think of you constantly. Damn it, you went and made me love you. But it'll never work. I have to give you up, and the sooner the better.*

"Susan, can we go for a drive?"

She shook her head. A tear escaped and slipped down her cheek. She feared that everyone had seen it. In fact, she felt like a freak on exhibition before the congregation's watchful eyes. "Home." It was the only word she could force around the knot forming in her throat.

The instant Eric stopped in her driveway, he enfolded her in his arms. "I'm so sorry, Susan. Please forgive me. I wish I'd never said what I did."

She wept uncontrollably, her tears wetting the fabric of his shirt. Inhaling deeply, she committed his scent to memory. Never, ever did she want to forget how wonderful he smelled up close. Her fingers caressed upward along his back, memorizing every muscle along the way. His neck, so smooth and warm. His hair, so soft and curling at his nape. His breath was moist on her neck. She prayed that she'd never forget how it felt, warming her heart and her soul.

He laughed softly and nuzzled her hair. "Does this mean you forgive me?"

Susan squeezed her eyes shut on the pain. "Yes...but I can't have you, Eric. I'm memorizing you."

"Nooo." His strong arms tightened around her. "Please, Susan. Say you don't mean that. Say you can't follow through. Say you love me too much."

She brushed her lips across his ear lobe and whispered, "I *do* love you. That's why I'm giving you up."

"No...please." His mouth murmured against her forehead. "I don't understand."

"All week I've let logic fly right out of my head. Tonight it returned. You're absolutely right, Eric. I can't be doing crazy things like that in public. It isn't appropriate. But don't you see? I've spent my life as I am. I'm independent. I'm spontaneous. I often say whatever comes to mind. I've never really cared what people might read into my words or actions. That's *their* problem."

"You're wonderful. I love you just the way you are."

"But I'm not raw material for a minister's wife. I know that sounds like I'm being presumptuous. But let's face it, you're not a man whose intentions would ever be dishonorable. When you started dating me, it was because you intended to propose if we were compatible. Am I right?"

"Yes."

"We're not compatible, Eric. You're deceiving yourself if you think that we are. I could never be the prim and proper minister's wife. If I were to host a ladies' circle, I'd have the elderly matrons aghast at my audacity."

"I don't believe that. You've grown up in this town. They already know you and love you."

She doubted that. "Okay. Try this one on then. What if you were to leave this parish and go somewhere else to serve? How would I fit into the new ladies' group?"

"You'd be a breath of fresh air that any group would be blessed to have."

She let the sweet words seep into every pore. How wonderful it would be if everyone could look at her as he did, through eyes blinded by love. He loved completely, and he fell into it quickly. Somewhere there was a woman who could be a better complement to his ministry than she could. She prayed that he'd move on soon and find that woman in another place—one where she wouldn't have to watch.

"How would that work, Eric? If you had to move to take another call, would you expect me to abandon everything I have here? I've worked my entire adult life building up my business." She felt him stiffen, and she squeezed her eyes on the pain that consumed her. *Oh Eric*, her mind screamed to speak. *I'd leave it all in a minute if I felt worthy of you.*

"Susan." Her name was spoken in anguish. A wet tear slid onto her cheek, and she knew it was his. "I'm so sorry. I never thought of what you'd be sacrificing. How could I be so selfish? Please forgive me."

Straightening, she dared to face him for one more unhindered study. His beautiful blue eyes were wet with remorse, the blonde lashes spiking. His hair curled around his ear. He reminded her of an angel—good, honest, kind. He would always put others ahead of himself when the chips were down. But he was also just naïve enough that he'd never realize her bluff. She cupped his cheek. It was smooth because he must have shaved for their ice cream. "Oh Eric," she whispered. "There's nothing to forgive."

Chapter 19

The past few days had been a test of the resiliency of the human spirit. Evelyn was grateful that her attendance was required at the library on Wednesday afternoon. The informational meeting for the reading volunteers was a welcome respite. She'd just finished Nell's second diary that morning, and she relished the well-timed dose of the here and now.

The diary had indeed been soul wrenching, but not at all in the way Evelyn had expected. Nell—the inner Nell, in her younger years—hadn't been the confident person that Evelyn had always imagined. She was fraught with insecurities, plagued with doubts, and drowning in low self-esteem. Deep inside, Nell was almost a replica of Evelyn at that age. They'd been Siamese twins, joined at the heart but with few outward characteristics that bore any resemblance at all.

Carl was the name of the man that Evelyn had never met. But Nell's vivid descriptions of his appearance and his soul, left Evelyn feeling as if she'd known him intimately. He wasn't at all the dandy that Evelyn had accused him of being. He was sincere, humble, and loved Nell with a love so pure that it was almost spiritual.

Nell and Carl had met at the library and were abiding friends long before they became lovers. They shared a passion for literature and would often discuss it over coffee after the library closed for the day. It was true that he was married and that his wife had left him. "She left me for a man with more money," he explained to Nell, "and I find that

I can't blame her. She's a woman who's accustomed to wealth, and I couldn't provide enough."

Yet Carl was a man of such principles that he had no intention of infidelity. It was only after he received papers that initiated the divorce proceedings that he even considered Nell in any light other than a friend. He procured his own attorney, signed the papers, and determined to get on with his life. And that life could only include Nell. Nell, who affirmed his sincerity, validated his worth, and loved him for who he was.

"It is true," Nell wrote then, "that the good men are taken, yet sadly neglected. Only those of us who waited too long seem able to appreciate them as they deserve. Carl has proposed, and I'll not wait a moment longer. Tonight I'll know him as a woman knows a man."

To read the account of that night as Nell described it was sheer poetry. It wasn't explicit in the carnal sense. But in the emotional realm, Evelyn had never read anything more graphically beautiful. Only Nell, with her acute sense of the soul, could have recorded a physical union in such a supernatural manner. "How could anyone but God have orchestrated such a symphony between his creatures—where a lowly man and woman could rise ever higher on the harmony until they touch His very face?" Evelyn wept to think that Nell had tasted such glory.

Then she wept again with the most overpowering grief as Nell was swept from heaven. Their world was shattered when Carl discovered that his attorney had misplaced the papers with which he'd been entrusted. And in the interim, his wife had reconsidered and refused the divorce. Evelyn found herself furious with Nell's acquiescence in the matter. Knowing Carl was a deeply religious man—a Catholic by faith—she recognized his deep commitment to God in his vows. "Perhaps it's a sign from God, Carl. He's given you a second chance to honor them. He's forgiven us for our indiscretions."

"How could you possibly label what we have as an *indiscretion*, Nell? Certainly in God's eyes, we are already married."

But in truth, Nell's well-honed habit of feeling herself to be unworthy, had come back to claim her. It rendered her virtually helpless to acknowledge that Carl could be right. And no one could understand better than Evelyn, just how persuasive Nell could be when she made up her mind. Carl hadn't had a prayer to dissuade her from her notion.

A week after Carl had tearfully departed, Evelyn had received Nell's shocking news and outlandish offer. If only she'd known the circumstances that had precipitated it, perhaps she might have been able to talk some sense into her. Evelyn would have used all her powers to try to persuade Nell to return to Carl. But of course, in her opinion, Carl was just a dandy.

"I will *not* claim your baby as my own, Nell. The very idea of it sounds scandalous, and I would *never* be a party to such deception."

Nell squared her shoulders. "All right then. I'll raise it myself. But please, Evelyn, will you help me to be a good mother? This baby deserves only the best, and if you won't raise it, would you at least help?"

How could Evelyn refuse such a desperate and tear-filled plea? She sighed wearily. "All right, Nell. I'll help you in any way I can."

In the ensuing weeks, Evelyn had never seen a happier Nell. She simply glowed with a maternal radiance, insisting that she would continue working as long as possible. "I don't understand how some women claim they're so tired when they're pregnant. I've never felt better."

Evelyn instantly became worried when Nell returned home from work just after lunch one day. "What's wrong, Nell? You don't look well."

"I think it's the flu. My stomach feels awful. I'm going to go lie down."

"Here, lean on me. I'll help you. We'll put you to bed and take your temperature. Maybe later you'll be able to eat a little soup."

"No...no soup. Nothing. I just want to lie down."

They had barely gained Nell's apartment when Nell doubled over in excruciating pain. Her friend's cries pierced Evelyn. She could almost feel the cramps herself.

"It's the baby!" Nell cried. "No God, please, please don't take my baby! Please don't take my baby!"

Nell's very spirit was snuffed out on that awful afternoon. She plunged into such devastating despair that, for months, Evelyn feared she might take her own life. Like a mother hen, she watched over her. As soon as her physical condition allowed, Evelyn encouraged her to go back to work. But only minimal improvement came to Nell's mental health by becoming gainfully employed once again. She returned to her lonely apartment each afternoon and insisted on cocooning herself within its confines.

Edward was supportive of Evelyn's ministrations to his sister. He often joined or took turns with her in keeping a watchful eye on Nell. They usually played cards or watched television or did whatever Nell seemed to prefer.

One night, five months after the miscarriage, Evelyn finally detected the tiniest spark of Nell's old zest for life. "We should have a party," she said as Edward dealt the cards.

Evelyn's eyes met her husband's, and she recognized her own hope within them. He winked. "Excellent idea. Evelyn, you and Nell should plan a party to end them all. The more the merrier, the louder the better. Let's see if we can all get evicted from this dump." They all laughed and began to plan.

Not long after that wonderful party, Evelyn awoke with nausea. The next morning was the same. And on the third, she finally dared to hope that her suspicions might be true. A doctor's test confirmed her fondest dream. She was pregnant.

Life was so unfathomable, Evelyn realized now. We struggle to attain what so often eludes us. Then suddenly find it dropped in our lap by the hand of God when we no longer expect it. But wasn't it odd that those unexpected gifts most often came when our energy was focused on helping those with greater needs than our own? On second thought, she decided, that wasn't odd at all. It was totally in character with God.

So it came to pass that Susan was born in May of the following year. There was never any question that Nell would be as involved in her nurturing as Evelyn was. Evelyn just hadn't counted on those trying teen years when she strongly suspected that Susan would have preferred that Nell be her natural mother. But after reading Nell's diary, Evelyn found it so easy to accept that small sacrifice. For hadn't Susan really come to be, only at the great price of Nell's tragic loss? And if not for Susan's idolization of her, would Nell have continued to heal?

Nell had included a few pages at the end of the diary, written only two years before her death, that proved how well she had mended. Those pages were the ones to which Hattie must have been referring when she told Evelyn that she'd be able to make peace with her past. Hattie had been absolutely right, and Evelyn decided to go to the nursing home on Wednesday evening to tell her so.

Hattie was talking animatedly with another woman when Evelyn arrived at her door. "C'mon in, Evie," she greeted her. "This is my new roommate, Irma. We're quite the pair, I tell you. They've given Irma a special name too. She's Irma the Instigator."

Evelyn extended her hand to the white-haired lady.

"Ah...Evie," Hattie warned. "I wouldn't do that if I were you. She's usually wired."

She snatched her hand back. "You mean they let you have those palm shocking devices in here?"

"No, of course not," Irma answered.

"She's got connections," Hattie added.

"Good heavens. And they actually let the two of you share the same room?"

"No one else will put up with either one of us." Hattie turned to Irma. "Scram for a while, would you? Evie and I need to talk privately for a few minutes."

"Oh, that's not necess—" Evelyn began.

"Don't worry," Hattie interrupted. "She's got a heist to pull in the storeroom anyway. Best if you don't ask any questions."

Irma managed to gain her feet, propped herself up with her cane, and waddled from the room.

"I see you've finished the diary."

"How did you know?" Evelyn took her usual seat beside her.

"The peace. I can see it in your face."

"You were right. It *did* resolve a lot of things I'd always had trouble forgiving myself for."

"She loved you."

"And I loved her. We were really so similar, despite our outward differences."

"No one's really that different inside. We all have the same needs...to feel loved and a reason for bein' here."

"Yes," Evelyn agreed. "Nell said it well. We are all worthy and have purpose simply because God created us. But it's through our relationships with others that He most often proves it to us."

"It's a downright shame that we sometimes hurt the ones we love most."

Evelyn nodded. "I hurt Edward so terribly during that awful time, shutting him out like that."

"But you came out of it with a stronger marriage in the end. Don't ever forget that."

"Yes. I realize that. It's the fire that tempers the steel."

Hattie leaned forward and studied her with interest. "What did you think of Nell's idea about the circle of life?"

"Very profound. You know, I never really understood what she meant by that expression until I read the diaries. She reasoned that chance, circumstances, and choices comprise the perimeter of our circles. But they all revolve around God, who works His will in the end, despite our attempts to thwart it."

"You kinda lost me there, Evie, with some of those words you used, but I understood it the way Nell wrote it down. Makes sense to me. I think she was right."

Evelyn agreed. There was a lot of comfort in believing that when you were trying to serve God, He was guiding you to the right harbor. "I'm also glad I understand why she was so bitter toward men for all those years. Carl sounded like such a wonderful man. I couldn't imagine why she'd become disillusioned after such a wonderful relationship."

"She had trouble forgivin' herself for letting him go. Blamed him for not fightin' her harder on that."

"But Nell was so persuasive. She finally understood that the blame belonged with her. And she found her peace in the idea of the circle...that things worked out in the end, the way God had intended all along."

"That *is* a comfortin' thought, ain't it?"

"Yes. It certainly helped me to forgive myself for all of my mistakes."

Hattie reached out and grasped Evelyn's hand. "I'm so glad you found your peace." She winked. "Now I s'pose you feel ready to meet your Maker."

She laughed, catching the gleam in her friend's eyes. "That's a funny thing, isn't it? When *does* a person ever feel ready to call it quits?"

"Ah...I figure some day we might. Seems to me that until you do, you must have some reason to keep on goin'."

Evelyn knew one of her reasons. Thoughts of Susan and the pastor had kept her hopeful throughout the stressful week. Susan hadn't told her too terribly much in her phone calls. But Evelyn just bet that if she'd see her face, it would be glowing. The two of them had gone for ice cream on Sunday evening, and he'd invited her to do the same tonight. Why, right now they were probably at the Dairy Queen. Two *dates* like that was definitely a promising sign. Once again, it seemed that God would answer her fondest request.

"Say, Evie. You don't have any Super Glue on you, do you?"

"Ah...no. I don't usually carry—"

"Shoot. Irma and I were gonna use it on the plastic shower caps."

"What plastic shower caps?"

"The ones she's gettin' out of the storeroom."

Evelyn shook her head. What a pair. They'd be evicted and homeless if they didn't watch their pranks. "I hate to ask, but what were you planning to make with the shower caps and Super Glue?"

"Whoopie cushions."

Irma waddled around the corner. "No shower caps. I struck out. They must be on to us."

"Shoot!" Hattie declared with a slap on her knee.

"But," Irma stated dramatically, leaning on her cane, "I found something else. Just lookie here." She unscrewed the handle on her walking stick and pulled a string from the hollow tube. "Ta da!" A plastic bag plooped out on the end of the line. "Balloons!"

"Balloons!" Hattie was excitedly clapping her hands. "That's even better!"

"Now you can have a party," Evelyn suggested.

"We sure can...as soon as we fill 'em with water. They'll understand. Can't expect old folks like us to have enough air to blow 'em up."

Irma nodded. "And the water's free."

Chapter 20

Eric wondered if he'd ever felt so lonely before. He must have, when he'd first learned of Kyle and Sharon's deaths. But as he drove home from Susan's house, he tried to figure out why the hollowness inside him felt so much more intense. He decided it must be because he'd been so incredibly happy just moments before everything had dropped out from under him. The past four days had been like a dream—the kiss, the phone calls, the second ice cream date. He'd been so certain that Susan was falling in love with him. And in fact, she'd just admitted that she was. Yet it wasn't enough. Who would've thought that love wasn't enough?

He suddenly realized that he sounded like a lovesick teenager. Of course love wasn't enough. Life was full of problems and complications. A nineteen-year-old would be naïve enough to think that love was enough. But a forty-three-year-old should know better. He'd been feeling just like a teenager all week. *That* was the problem. And it had been wonderful. Romantic love was so powerful—especially new love. It knocked you right out of the real world.

Since it was only eight o'clock, he decided to stop at his best friend's place. Who else could you share your burdens with? Well, there was God of course, but Eric didn't feel that patient. Tonight he needed to talk to someone who could give him some input right away.

"She's bluffing," Marcus said after Eric had explained the whole series of events. He sat behind his study desk with his feet propped up on the blotter. That usually annoyed Eric because Marcus' tennis shoes were always dirty. They were no different now, but Eric enjoyed the normalcy of his friend's posture. The world *was* still orbiting the sun.

"Bluffing? Why would you say that?"

"She licked you."

Eric reddened. "Yeah. So what? I don't see how you can put that with anything and come up with *bluffing*."

"Okay, it was *that* plus some other details that I thought you'd be too embarrassed for me to repeat. Like the way she *memorized* you, for example. *That* certainly doesn't sound like someone who really wanted to give you up so easily. Then of course there's your ridiculous blunder at the Dairy Queen. I mean, man, Eric, she just licked you. She didn't rip your shirt off or anything."

He bit back his anger. Maybe immediate input hadn't been the best way to go. God would've been better. "I realize that I overreacted there."

"You sure did. So now the poor woman's imagining all kinds of things. Like what an embarrassment she'd be to you if the two of you were to hook up, how she'd drag your ministry down, probably get you booted right out of the parish."

"That's ridiculous."

"Of *course* it's ridiculous, but *that's* how women think."

"How did *you* get to be such an expert?"

"Don't wanna go there, buddy. Let's get back on track. *You're* the one with the problem, remember?"

How could he forget? The hollowness was a dull ache. "Okay. Let's assume you're right. What can I do about it now?"

Marcus stroked his chin for a long time. At least he was giving the question some honest thought. He sighed. "Wow, Eric. That's a tough one. How ethical do you wanna be?" Eric glared at him. Marcus upended his palms in surrender. "Okay, okay. *Very* ethical. Well, you could try the direct approach. Go over to see her and call her bluff."

He considered that scenario. "I don't think it would work. For one thing, she's stubborn. And then there's the fact that she believes that string of bologna in the first place...what you said about being an embarrassment to me and stuff. I mean, if she really *believes* that, how can I possibly change her mind?"

They both sat in silence for several long minutes. "I'm drawing a blank here, Eric. Why don't you give me a couple days, and I'll see if I can come up with any other ideas."

"All right," he agreed as he rose. "Thanks a lot. I appreciate it."

"No problem. That's what friends are for."

Eric turned at the doorway. "Just out of curiosity, what would your unethical suggestion have been?"

"That's easy. Tell everyone you're putting out feelers for a new parish. I mean, right now she probably wishes you'd leave town so she doesn't have to face you." He grinned, tapping his fingertips together. "But I'll just bet if she *really* thought you were leaving, she'd come chasing after you."

Eric gaped. "You *are* crazy. You'd actually suggest that I jerk all the people in my congregation around like that, on the chance that it would make Susan see reason?"

"Hey, it was just an idea. Can't blame a guy for thinking."

That had been a dead end, Eric decided on his way home. But at least he'd sensed some real sympathy in his friend's eyes when he'd told him the story. It felt better when you shared your sorrow with someone who cared, even if their ideas weren't the best.

Eric spent most of Thursday trying to keep busy, but Susan still controlled his thoughts. John stopped over after work to say goodbye. He was going to be packing that evening and flying out on Friday. It would have been a very difficult parting for Eric if he hadn't known that his brother would be back by the end of the year. The thought reminded Eric of another reason why Marcus' unethical idea had been so ridiculous. Who would believe that he was interested in changing parishes when his brother's family would soon be moving to town?

"Tell me what's going on between you and Susan," John said.

"Nothing...anymore."

"That's what I figured."

"Why?"

"At the beginning of the week she was walking around in a daze. Someone told me they'd seen the two of you at the Dairy Queen. Then today she was...I don't know...kinda moping around."

"Moping? Really?" He realized that he sounded pathetically desperate, but the news gave him hope.

"Why don't you tell me what happened."

Eric did and by doing so, found a bit more of his burden lifted. John agreed with Marcus concerning Susan's likely motives for rejecting him. But he didn't have any suggestions for putting Eric's world back together.

"Hang in there, Eric," he said as they hugged goodbye. "These things have a way of working out if they're meant to be." Eric felt a real encouragement by his words. And after John had left, he realized why. For the first time that he could remember, his brother had initiated the hug. It had been warm and genuine.

On Friday Marcus called to say that he hadn't come up with any other ideas. Eric knew he had to begin writing his sermon. But for most of the morning as he sat at his desk, pen in hand, his thoughts drifted to his marriage to Sharon. She'd been so different from Susan. How was it possible to love two women who were so dissimilar? In fact, in some ways they were almost opposites. Sharon had been quiet and demure; Susan was outgoing and wasn't afraid to speak her mind. Sharon had seemed perfectly satisfied with full-time homemaking; Susan needed the challenge of an outside career. He loved the stimulating conversations that he and Susan had. He had never done that with Sharon. It was terrible to admit, but he realized that Sharon would no longer satisfy him if she were to magically reappear in his life.

Was that thought a sin from which he should repent? he wondered. Certainly if Sharon had never died he wouldn't feel that way. They would have spent all that time since, growing closer. Instead he'd been forced to spend the time growing accustomed to being alone. He'd learned to do many of the things himself that Sharon used to do—the laundry, light housekeeping, school conferences. And Kim had been forced to become more independent and responsible too. Eric decided that the circumstances had forced him to change, and that's why Susan held more appeal to him now. That wasn't a sin. It was a sign that he'd grown and come to accept his new life.

Once again, Eric was reminded of the depression that Sharon had battled. It seemed obvious to him now that she hadn't really been happy with her life. Had she wished for an outside career perhaps? He wished that she had discussed it with him. Had she wished that he would help her more? Listen to her more? Understand her more? Appreciate her more? He honestly couldn't rule out any of those possibilities.

Their marriage had been good, but it could have been so much better. They'd both fallen into the habit of using each other, in a way. Eric had always tried to be considerate. But when he'd needed to ask Sharon for extra assistance, like hosting a council meeting, he'd been extra polite or appreciative. He was stunned to realize that he'd been kissing up, trying to solicit her cooperation. He felt such shame. It was very likely that he was partly to blame for her depression.

Eric bowed his head at his desk and asked God to forgive him. It hadn't been intentional, but it had been wrong. Somewhere along the line, he'd forgotten that Sharon had been a special gift. She had once knocked him out of the real world just as Susan had so recently done. But then he'd grown accustomed to Sharon, taken her for granted. And he'd forgotten the most important job that God had given him in marriage. He should have been trying to make his wife feel secure and significant—not because it would benefit him, but because it would have made God more real to her.

He raised his head and stared at his blank legal pad before him. He'd gotten off track again and hadn't begun to write his sermon.

Then suddenly he realized that *marriage* would be the perfect subject for a sermon. It didn't exactly follow the liturgy for the week, but a deviation was acceptable now and then. And he also decided that he'd tell the congregation about his wife and his son. It was high time they got to know them too.

When Eric stepped out to welcome everyone on Sunday morning, the first person he looked for was Susan. Her mother sat in her customary place, but she was alone. He tried to hide his disappointment, but he suspected that Mrs. Justison could see right through him. Later in the service, he led the congregation in the Gospel reading. Then he began the sermon that he'd put so much heart into preparing. It seemed almost pointless now, since the one person he'd prepared it for wasn't even present.

"It's been a soul-searching week for me, and I hope you won't mind if I deviate from the Gospel today in order to share some of my discoveries with you."

They all seemed intrigued by his introduction so he continued, feeling more relaxed. "We're all blessed to have special friends with whom we can bear our souls. They're really gifts from God. They can be honest with us and sometimes point out areas in which we've become disillusioned about ourselves. We can accept their suggestions, because we know that they love us and only want what's best for us. This week I shared something with my friend that I haven't shared with anyone else in Crow River, and I came out of the encounter healed."

Eric went on to tell them about the accident, Kyle and Sharon, and the cleansing sense of having his guilt over the incident assuaged. He kept it brief and to the point. But perhaps since his confessions were of such a personal nature, he detected more interest in the congregation. Even Mr. Oldenberg was staying awake. It was too bad Susan wasn't there to see that.

"I'd like those of you who are married to try to recall how you felt when you first realized you were in love. Euphoric? As though all was right with the world? As though you were somehow walking in another reality? Perhaps you felt like you were dreaming." He continued with confession that he had felt the same way early on in his marriage. But during his soul-searching of the past week, he'd realized that he hadn't always been the husband he could have been.

"It occurred to me that what we often label as 'taking our spouse for granted' is actually something else. It is in fact, our losing sight of our primary purpose in a marriage. Our spouse is another soul that God has entrusted to our care. Marriage is indeed the most intimate of human relationships. It's our one chance on earth to show another human being the totality of God's love."

A bit more elaboration was needed so Eric did so. But again, he kept it brief and to the point. "So in conclusion, I urge those of you who are married to take a few moments this afternoon to really speak to your husband or wife. Share your dreams openly with one another. But don't do so with the attitude that 'this is what *you* could do for *me* in order to make my life happier.' Instead, your primary goal should be to listen, to ask yourself what *you* can do for this one special person that God has entrusted to your care. We never know when they'll be taken from us. I truly believe that the strongest marriages are those that are a partnership in which the other is put first. When *both* partners concentrate on this goal, they'll make the most astounding discovery possible. For they'll find that their *own* needs...for love, for significance...have somehow been magically met in the process."

It hadn't been a phenomenal sermon, Eric decided as he stood shaking hands in the receiving line. But it had seemed to hold their attention. Most of the comments seemed positive anyway. As the last person filed past, he wondered where Mrs. Justison had gone. He'd been looking for her. But when he returned to his church office to remove his vestment, he found her waiting in his guest chair.

"I hope you'll forgive my forwardness, Pastor, but I take it things didn't go as well with Susan as you'd hoped."

"Is she all right?" he asked as he hung up his robe. "I...I was hoping to see her here today."

The woman waved her hand dismissively. "I'm sure she's fine. She called me this morning to tell me she was feeling a little under the weather. But judging from your sermon, I've guessed that it might be more of an emotional ailment."

Eric took the other chair beside her. He sighed. "I'm sure you're right." He went on, in minimal detail, to explain how the week had unfolded. "I think I managed to scare her off," he concluded.

She patted his knee briefly, then folded her hands together in her lap, a satisfied smile on her face. "Oh, I wouldn't say all's lost. It sounds like you managed to shake her up a bit. That's very encouraging. She must be terribly fond of you."

He reddened. He certainly wasn't going to tell her mother that Susan had confessed her love. "I'm very fond of her too."

"Then I think it will all work out. I'd planned on going over there this afternoon to see how she's feeling." Her face held a scheming expression.

"You won't...ah...mention that we talked or anything, will you?" He certainly hoped not. He doubted that would sit well with Susan.

She laughed. "Please, Pastor, give me a bit more credit than that. Susan wouldn't take *that* well at all. No, some things are better left unspoken." She rose and turned back to him, a cagey smile in place. "But don't worry. I have a couple aces up my sleeve."

Eric stood as she retrieved her handbag and started for the door. Suddenly she turned back and enfolded him in a brief but warm hug. It was a surprise, but somehow it felt right. And as he smiled down into her eyes, he felt hopeful for the first time in days.

Chapter 21

Susan was lying on her couch, enshrouded in a blanket, when her mother dropped by on Sunday afternoon. It wasn't a surprise. She knew she'd stop over to see how she was. Even Peanut and Princess were so used to her mother's visits under such circumstances that they paid her no mind. Princess was nestled under Susan's arm, and Peanut's head rested on her feet.

"Are you feeling better, honey?" she asked as she took a seat in the tufted chair beside the sofa.

"A little, but I decided to take tomorrow off. Marvin said he could handle it, and I think I could use the rest." Susan reassured herself that she wasn't actually lying. Her emotions had worn her energy level down to the minimum.

"Pastor Masterson gave a wonderful sermon this morning. Apparently he had a son who he lost in the accident that killed his wife. He talked to a special friend this week who had helped him heal."

Susan felt a lump form in her throat. At least she'd been able to help him sort through that. "Sounds like it must've been kind of a depressing sermon."

"Oh, not at all. He said he'd been doing a lot of thinking about his wife during the week, and he realized that he hadn't been as good a husband as he could have been. Then he launched into a beautifully inspiring essay on what makes a good marriage."

Susan sat up. Princess protested a little as she was pushed aside, then found a place to curl up on the back of the couch. Susan didn't know what to think of his sermon topic, but she felt the sharp piercing of jealousy. Apparently her rejection had made Eric somewhat relieved in the end. To think, he'd spent the end of the week remembering his wife. All she'd been able to think about was him. She wanted to cry.

"Are you all right, dear?"

"Fine," she lied and decided she'd have to do a better job of appearing unaffected. "So what did he say makes a good marriage?"

"I thought it was very profound. He obviously put a lot of thought into it. He said that our spouse is a special gift from God. We should love them unselfishly, not expecting them to meet *our* needs, but by concentrating on meeting *their* needs. By doing so, he said, we'd magically discover that our own needs would be met after all."

"Sounds complicated."

"Love always is. My, you should've seen the struggles your father and I went through...especially before you were born."

"You must mean when you lived in San Francisco. Nell mentioned it was kind of a rough time."

"The roughest...for all of us. In fact, I've only just this past week come to terms with it myself. There are things that happened there that I've never dared to share with you."

She felt a shiver race down her spine. "Y...You didn't have an affair or something, did you, Mom?"

She laughed. "Heavens no. But Nell did."

Susan was flabbergasted. She did a double take to make sure her mother had spoken the words. She had. "Okay, you threw me for a real loop there, Mom. Can you tell me about it?"

Reaching into her oversized bag, she extracted two leather books and handed them to her. "I think Nell's words do more justice to the story than mine ever could."

Susan studied the worn volumes in her hand and opened one. "This...this looks like her diary."

"It is. I think you'd benefit from reading it. The one you have there is the first one. Best to start at the beginning."

She had a sudden discomforting thought. "This isn't like...porn, is it? I don't think I could handle that very well. I mean, she was my aunt and all."

Her mother laughed. "If it's pornographic, it's certainly the most poetic pornography *I've* ever read."

Susan dived into the diary as soon as her mother left. In truth, she was not only intrigued, but grateful for the distraction from her own problems. In no time, she was carried away by Nell's vivid description of their trip and their arrival. The people that Nell met seemed to almost come off the pages. Susan could envision the library where she worked and her daily routine. Nell's characteristic attention to the smallest details made it captivating.

The doorbell chimed at seven o'clock, just as she'd finished the first volume. Peanut started making a ruckus, so Susan put him out when she answered the summons. Kimberly stood on the step.

"Hi Susan. Are you feeling better?"

"A little. Come on in and keep me company for a while." She held the door for her and then went back to her bed on the couch. "Have a seat," she told the girl. Kim sat down in the chair her mother had taken earlier. "What's up?"

Kim sighed. "I think my dad's looking for a new wife."

Susan tried very hard not to let any emotion show on her face. "Why do you think that?"

"He gave a sermon this morning on marriage. So this afternoon I asked him why."

She sat up more attentively, pushing Princess out of the way. "And what did he say?"

"He said he'd been doing a lot of thinking this week about my mom. He realized that he'd grown and changed a lot since she died. And if she were to come back, they probably wouldn't be compat...com—"

"Compatible?"

"Yeah. *Compatible* anymore. Then he said that if he *did* marry again, my new mother would probably be someone who had another job. He wanted to know if that would bother me."

"Would it?"

"No. I've changed a lot too. I like taking care of things around the house. I told him I wouldn't want someone moving in and changing everything again."

Susan felt a clenching around her heart. Apparently Eric intended to do just what she'd hoped and find a wife more suitable. She certainly couldn't blame him, but it still hurt. At least he wouldn't be lonely. She just wished she wouldn't have to watch it. "What if you have to move? Would that bother you?"

"He never asked me about that. If he had, I would've told him I don't want to move. I like Crow River."

Great, Susan thought. "Oh, but if your dad fell in love with someone, Kim, wouldn't you be willing to move if you knew it would make him happier?"

She thought about that awhile. "I don't know. Maybe. But I wouldn't really want to."

"Sometimes we have to do things we don't like if we love someone."

Kim sighed. "I guess." She sat there staring at Susan for a long while.

"Was there something else you wanted to say, honey?"

"No. I just needed to talk to someone about it, and you're my best older friend."

Susan felt tears welling up. "That's so sweet, honey. You're my best *younger* friend too." Kim bounded off the chair and wrapped her arms around her. Susan squeezed back and let a few tears seep out. Oh, how badly she wished things could be different.

"Thanks, Susan. I feel better."

"Me too," she lied.

Kim pulled away with a smile on her face to prove her claim. Susan tried to fake one of her own. "I'd better let you rest again."

Susan watched her leave before letting Peanut inside, then decided that chocolate was in order—lots of it. So she raided the kitchen and produced a bag of chocolate chips. Thus armed, she returned to the couch to begin volume two of Nell's story.

For several hours, she turned pages, entranced. She'd had no idea she had been so wanted by her mother and father. She'd had no idea how lonely her aunt Nell had been. An entirely new perspective of her mother, father, and aunt unfolded before her very eyes. A tissue box replaced the chocolate chips, and she dived into it just as frequently. At midnight she turned the final page and sat spellbound, trying to process all she'd read.

How tragic. The story of Carl and Nell was as poignant as Romeo and Juliet. No...more so, because at any time Nell could have tried to find him again but never did. Susan had never dreamed that Nell had once thought so little of herself. Nell had been Susan's idol all her life. But of course by the time Susan had grown, Nell had probably already been resolving those inner issues. Her outer confidence had never seemed lacking in any way.

Susan found herself a little angry with Nell for sending Carl back to his wife. The very idea that Nell didn't think he'd be happy with her seemed preposterous. Nell was wonderful, exuberant. Any man would've been better off with her.

Suddenly Susan smelled a rat with her mother's name on it. Why had her mother waited all these years to share this with her? Why now, when she was facing some similar issues, would her mother choose to drop this in her lap? Fate? Not likely, considering her mom had begun her whole campaign with all that stuff about Eric's wonderful marriage sermon. So that left only one option—her mother suspected what was going on with her.

But did it matter? Not really, she decided. Obviously, her mom just wanted to spare her from a similar fate. So the question was, had any of this changed Susan's opinion? She gave the question great consideration and had to admit that it had.

The truth of the matter was that she loved Eric. She'd thrown him away because (what had she said?) she wasn't good *raw material* for a minister's wife. Had she actually *said* that? Did love make a person stupid or something? She was Susan Justison, and she'd been fighting uphill battles all her life. She could be the very best at whatever she chose to tackle. And if she wanted to be a minister's wife, she could damn well handle it properly!

She reasoned that the first thing she'd have to do would be to exorcise words like *damn* from her thought vocabulary. In the pickup on the way over to Eric's, she reasoned that the second thing she'd have to remember in the future would be to schedule visits of this type for a more appropriate time.

A light was still on in an upstairs bedroom when she pulled in his driveway. Susan killed the engine and hopped out. She hesitated a moment on the porch, wondering what she should say. Before she could knock, the inner door swung open. Eric stood behind the screened one. He was tousled, shirtless, and dressed only in jeans from the waist down. He looked fabulous.

"Are you just going to stare?" he asked.

"Do you have a problem with that?"

He grinned. "Not really, but I suppose I should put on my shirt before I invite you in." He left for a moment and returned, buttoning it up. "C'mon in." He held the door while she slipped past, then closed it. When he turned back, they stood transfixed, gazing into each other's eyes.

"I missed you," she whispered.

Relief spread across his face. "I missed you too." He closed the distance and enfolded her in a full hug.

He smelled delicious, and she reveled in the warmth. "Heard you might be scouting around for a wife." She mumbled the words against his shirt.

"Could be. Are you applying?"

"Possibly. If you're still taking applications." She felt his Adam's apple move as he swallowed.

"It's not an advertised opening. How did you hear about it?"

"Kim came by this afternoon to talk. She was kind of worried about it after your sermon and your talk with her afterwards."

"Let's sit down and discuss things." He pulled away and led her by the hand to a kitchen chair. There he scooped her up and sat down, settling her comfortably on his lap. "I thought I'd never be able to hold you like this again."

"You've *never* held me like this."

"Not in reality...no. But in my dreams...many times."

She quirked her head. "Really? Have you had any other dreams?"

He smiled, looking a little embarrassed. "Maybe."

"Ah...so *that's* how it's going to be, huh? I'll have to be fighting you for every scrap of information." She ruffled his soft hair. Their eyes met, and they both tipped their heads. "I love you, Eric," she whispered just before their lips touched.

"I love you, Susan." He breathed the words amid feathered kisses. Then he deepened the kiss like before, and Susan could feel herself drowning again. He tasted so perfect—strength and gentleness all rolled into one man. They ever so slowly returned to the surface. He tucked her head in the crook of his neck. "We were going to talk."

"Mmm hmm."

"How did I get so lucky as to have you change your mind?"

Susan told him about Nell's diaries that her mother had brought over. "And I realized I was angry at Nell for being such a chicken. Then I realized that I was probably being the same way."

"It doesn't hurt to be cautious. Marriage *is* a big step. It's not always easy, and it lasts all your life."

"Do you think I could be a good minister's wife?"

"Do you think I could be a good carpenter's husband?"

She laughed. "Not fair...answering a question with a question."

"I know. I only meant that each of us probably feels the same way. I'm scared that I won't measure up to your expectations. And you're scared that you won't measure up to mine."

"What *are* your expectations?" She lifted her head to watch him think.

"It's really too early to say, Susan. We haven't known each other long enough. I think the longer we know each other, the more likely our expectations will align with reality. Does that make sense?"

"Perfect sense. So we should date for a while then. And if we decide to become engaged, we should plan on a reasonable length for an engagement. And of course there's always the possibility that we'll decide we're not right for each other."

"Do you think so?"

"No. But we shouldn't feel obligated or something if one of us should change their mind."

"I agree." He patted her knee. "So that's the plan then...first we date to see how it goes."

"Wait. There's also Kim to consider here. I mean, if we should date, she might get her hopes up and—"

"Assume that we'll get married."

"Yes. So that will be something we'll have to explain to her."

Kim popped excitedly around the corner, shocking them both almost onto the floor. "I understand!" she exclaimed with a squeal at the end and wrapped her arms around them both.

When the warm, joyous moment had passed, Eric put on a serious expression. "Kim," he chastised. "Were you eavesdropping?"

"Yes."

"Shouldn't you apologize?"

"I suppose. But shouldn't you thank me?"

"For what?"

"For going over to Susan's and scaring her into believing you might want to date someone else."

"You mean you *planned* that?"

"Yep." Her blonde hair tumbled around her face. Her bare toes protruded beneath the hem of her nightgown as she stood, beaming a proud smile. "Pretty good, huh? In poker, it's called *bluffing*."

Eric shook his head wearily. "Ah...yes. I can see this is going to be...interesting."

Susan couldn't agree more. Another challenge had been passed her way. Very likely the biggest one she'd ever had. If things worked out, in a few months she'd be a wife and a mother—the two biggest jobs in the world. She should have felt frightened but she didn't. In fact, she'd never felt more ready to tackle them. But then, she'd never been more certain that God was in her corner either.

Chapter 22

▼

The April morning had begun dreary and rainy almost a year after Nell had been buried. But by noon the sun had smiled in all its glory. And by three o'clock when the wedding ceremony began, it had chased away every cloud in the blue sky.

Eric and Susan made a beautiful couple—he in his black tuxedo and she in her pearl embroidered gown. John and Marcy Masterson were their best man and matron of honor. They'd moved to Crow River in December and had recently acquired the parsonage that John intended to modernize. Their oldest son Jeb, and Kimberly were the junior attendants. Joshua, their youngest, had read the scripture and had done a fine job. Cindy Gunderson had fussed over Susan, taking her personal attendant duties seriously. And Father Marcus had been granted special permission to officiate at the marriage of his friends.

The groom had been surprised when they'd exited the sanctuary into the traditional rain of rice confetti. Crepe paper streamers adorned a sporty car that he didn't recognize. Evelyn overheard him ask Susan, "Did you rent a Mustang for today?"

"No," she responded, smiling proudly. "It's your wedding gift from me."

"My wedding gift!" He lowered his voice. "Susan, I'm a little embarrassed. I didn't spend nearly as much on your gift."

"Sure you did. The honeymoon cost is comparable to my down payment on the car. But I'm afraid you'll have to make the thirty-six easy payments."

He flushed, running his finger inside his collar beneath the bow tie. "And where do you propose I get the money for the thirty-six easy payments?"

"Shh, Eric. Keep your voice down." Heeding her own advice, she lowered hers to the barest whisper. Evelyn had to lean in to hear. "You can use the housing allowance you'll be getting. My house is paid for, so you won't need it for that."

His brows knit. "That sounds a little unethical."

"Do you like the car?"

"I love it. But red? Do you really think red is appropriate for a—?"

"Eric, get over it. Live a little."

Evelyn and Hattie rode with John and Marcy's family in their minivan to the reception. Apparently Susan had time to unruffle her husband's feathers during the drive to the country club. He emerged from his new car looking carefree and entirely at peace with the world.

"You've got lipstick on your collar," John told him as Eric held the passenger door open for his bride.

The boyish smile faded until Susan procured something from her purse that eradicated the problem.

"Land sakes," Hattie said as Evelyn wheeled her into the banquet room. "I'm gonna enjoy watching that girl of yours rock his world."

"You've been doing a fine job of it yourself today."

Evelyn was referring to Hattie's earlier stunt. The white runner had been unfurled down the center aisle of the church to reveal a nasty surprise. The words "Help me!" had been markered onto the paper runway with an arrow pointing toward Susan.

Hattie had snorted beside Evelyn in the front pew.

"How did you manage *that*?" Evelyn scolded her.

"I found a nice young man to help me."

"And I suppose you used your *helpless* routine again."

"Beggars can't be choosers, Evie. We gotta use whatever means is available to us."

"Honestly, your husband must have had his hands full. What did he do for a living?"

"August? He was a minister."

My, Evelyn wished she'd been armed with that information earlier. It would've provided added leverage to use on Susan during those unsettling days of almost a year past. But she was cleansed to know that she'd shared Nell's diary with her daughter. They had several heart-to-heart discussions after Susan had read it, and the sharing had made them even closer.

Later, however, Susan had gotten a hair-brained notion to try to locate Nell's Carl. Evelyn had tried to dissuade her from such a venture. As usual, her arguments had fallen on deaf ears. But that had worked out well in the end too. Now Evelyn was glad that Susan had been so stubborn.

Susan had located the man six months ago and had been corresponding with him quite regularly. The biggest surprise was to learn that he and Nell had been writing to each other as well. Every few years, they'd exchanged a long letter. It was odd that Evelyn had never found Carl's letters among Nell's things. But Nell had likely committed them to memory and discarded them.

Carl and his wife had slowly rebuilt their marriage into a strong and enduring one. They were blessed with one child—a daughter who had two children of her own. His wife had just passed away shortly before Susan had contacted him. He took the news of Nell's death quite hard, but his communication with Susan seemed to be helping him heal. Three months ago, Susan asked her permission to send Carl the diaries. How could Evelyn refuse? Nell's diaries belonged with him.

Now the buffet reception was proceeding beautifully. The banquet room had been prepared for three hundred guests. It was terribly difficult to keep the guest list reasonable when the groom was a minister. Evelyn reasoned that almost the entire congregation was present.

Eric's parents and their grandson Joshua shared the table with Evelyn and Hattie. Mr. Masterson had teased Evelyn at the rehearsal dinner the evening before. "It's getting lonely in Chicago. I don't know what Minnesota's got that's so special. But now it's taken my other boy and my grandchildren away."

She felt particularly clever as she responded. "It must be the women."

He scratched his head. "Well, I see what you mean with Eric, but how do you figure that with John?"

"They make better employers," she quipped.

Mr. Masterson guffawed, and they'd been getting along famously ever since.

The rising tinkle of flatware tapping on glassware forced Eric and Susan to stand from their seats behind the head table. This had been the fifth time, and Eric looked like he was running out of patience. He dramatically swept down over Susan, leaning her back over his arm and upsetting her veil. The kiss went on and on.

"Good heavens," Hattie said while fanning herself. "That boy can kiss like August."

"I taught him everything he knows," Eric's father stated proudly.

To which his mother responded with a teasing rebuke. "You have one chance to restate that claim."

"I taught him *almost* everything he knows."

"That's better."

The couple finally came up for air. Susan stooped to retrieve her veil from the floor. Eric made the good-natured announcement, "Enough, everyone. No more please."

"Amen," Hattie murmured. "Any more of that, and they'll both melt."

The dance began once the meal was completed. Evelyn smiled dreamily as the bride and groom performed a flawless waltz alone on the floor. Soon the bridal party and other guests joined them, and the room was softly swirling with the graceful flow of the ladies' colorful skirts. Hattie and Evelyn occupied themselves with comments on the day and the dancers. A short while later, Eric appeared and gallantly requested that Evelyn dance with him.

"Thank you, Mrs. Justison," he told her as he guided her effortlessly, "for all you did to make Susan see reason."

"Shh," she cautioned with a smile. "Not so loudly. *See reason* wouldn't sit too well with Susan. And I think you can call me Evelyn now."

"You're absolutely right, Evelyn." He smiled down at her. "So tell me, how are you and the cat getting along?"

Evelyn had inherited Princess. Susan had brought her over the night before. "Just fine. I like having her around. She's good company."

"Good. I'm glad she got a nice home."

"Just out of curiosity, was it Princess who scratched your nose a long while back?"

He reddened. "Ah no. It was Peanut."

"Oh. I certainly hope you two will get along now."

"One can only hope."

The waltz ended soon after, and Eric escorted her back to Hattie. A moment later, Susan appeared on the arm of an older gentleman who seemed vaguely familiar. He was about six feet tall, of a very trim build, and still sported a rather full head of graying hair. It had faded from red to a bronze.

"Mom? I'd like you to meet a special friend of mine who flew in for the wedding. This is Nell's friend, Carl. This is my mom, Evelyn."

Within moments, she'd handed him over and gone off to greet other guests. Evelyn felt breathless as he took a seat beside her. Hattie couldn't close her mouth.

"You both seem shocked," he said with a grin.

Evelyn found her voice. "Well…yes. It's just such a surprise. Susan hadn't told me a thing."

"Actually, I wasn't sure I'd be able to make it, so I hadn't responded to her invitation. I only just now found it appropriate to introduce myself to her."

"I see. Well, it's wonderful that you could come here today, Carl." Evelyn wished Hattie would close her mouth or at least use it to say something.

"Sooo...you're Carl." Hattie finally spoke. Evelyn wanted to kick her under the table.

He reddened slightly. "Yes, I'm Carl. Susan warned me that you've both read Nell's diaries. So we might as well dispense of that topic right away."

"Oh, please don't feel uncomfortable. I, for one, found Nell's diaries to be absolutely beautiful. I mean, she wrote so beautifully and, as you know, that was a terribly painful period for me. So I think to find the diaries beautiful...well, that says—"

"A lot for the writer."

"Oh yes. And the relationship, I think."

He smiled warmly. "Thank you...may I call you Evelyn?" She nodded. "Thank you, Evelyn."

"And I'm Hattie." Her friend stuck her hand between them, and he shook it.

"Ah yes. Nell wrote me about you too. It's very nice to meet two of her closest friends."

The conversation gradually grew more relaxed. Carl told them that his oldest granddaughter had recently married a man from Minnesota and now lived in the twin cities. Evelyn told him that she'd recently started working three afternoons a week at the public library. Hattie told him about some of her nursing home pranks. By the end of the evening, they were laughing together like old friends.

"Would you care to dance, Evelyn? It's the last one."

"I'd love to dance." She smiled. "But please don't say *it's the last one.*"

"Allow me to amend my statement." Carl extended his arm to escort her. "It's the last one *of the evening*."

"I like the sound of that much better."

She allowed him to lead her until they reached the center, where he faced her, offering his hand. Soon they were gliding around the floor, comfortably enjoying the gentle flow of the waltz and the partners surrounding them. The subdued lighting was like twilight, and Evelyn couldn't help but be reminded that she was in her twilight years. Tomorrow she'd likely sleep a bit later and awaken stiff from just the small exertion of this dance. But how different her attitude was from a year ago. Then, she'd been preparing to die. Now, she was content to live for however long God ordained. And she realized that every point along the circle of life was really a beginning. For circles never end.

About the Author

Christine Paul lives in Minnesota and enjoys making people laugh. The high school valedictorian and college honors graduate writes to entertain and enlighten. In *The Circle of Life*, her believable characters question their purpose and will capture your heart and soul in their quest.

0-595-22870-4